SKETCHES AND TALES

OF THE

SHETLAND ISLANDS.

SKETCHES AND TALES

OF THE

SHETLAND ISLANDS.

BY

ELIZA EDMONDSTON.

———◆———

Fredonia Books
Amsterdam, The Netherlands

Sketches and Tales of the Shetland Islands

by
Eliza Edmondston

ISBN: 1-4101-0239-4

Reprinted from the 1856 edition

Fredonia Books
Amsterdam, The Netherlands
http://www.fredoniabooks.com

CONTENTS.

CHAPTER VIII.

CONTENTS

vii

CHAPTER XIX

CHAPTER XX

CHAPTER XXI

SKETCHES AND TALES

OF THE

SHETLAND ISLANDS.

CHAPTER I.

GENERAL SKETCH OF SHETLAND.

IT is not a great while ago, that a young gentleman from the Shetland Islands, arrived in
London, for the purpose of prosecuting the profession to which he was destined. He was invited
one day to dine with a small party, at the house of
an attached friend of his family. The youth had
never before been absent from his home; public
life, with all its tumults and conventionalities, was
new to him, and it cannot be wondered at, that he
was reserved and somewhat sad.

After the cloth had been removed his kind
hostess endeavoured to amuse and interest him, by
asking questions about his island home. When he
had replied to them, a general officer who was present, and had been attending to the slight conversation, addressed him politely—" *Pray, Sir, where
is Shetland ?* "

The colour mounted to the cheek and brow

A

of the sensitive young stranger. He was taken quite by surprise; and asked himself, was this question put by way of sneer or banter? The gentleman-like deportment and benevolent countenance of the querist would not permit such a suspicion. His beloved rocky fatherland was therefore quite unknown to this gentleman of rank and education! The youth's embarrassment was but momentary, yet a slight shade of astonishment and formality might be detected mingling with the gentle suavity of his general demeanour, as he replied, " Shetland is the name given to a group of islands in the Northern Atlantic, about 150 miles north of Britain."

We trust there are few of our readers who require this piece of information now-a-days, when locomotion, and consequent intelligence are so rife. Yet still, we believe, Shetland is but little known; its very name is apt to be mistaken. Sir Walter Scott, in " The Pirate," rendered *Zetland*, the classical orthography, and in this form it now gives title to an earldom. But *Zetland* is a corruption of a comparatively modern Scotch, or rather Dutch name—*Yetland;* Z being sounded as Y, especially in proper names. *Shetland* is the more ancient, and better known appellative; it is also the vernacular *pronunciation*, whatever *spelling* be adopted; and it is, by the natives generally, and we think, very properly preferred. Should, however, veritable *antiquity* give a name a preferable title to general adoption, *Hialtland* can boast such pre-eminence, as in this form it is found in the Icelandic Sagas.

The general aspect, scenery, and customs of these islands, are so different, from aught that British travellers are accustomed to meet with, we trust some brief sketches tending to delineate and illustrate them, will not be unwelcome in these palmy days for tourists; the more especially, as a complete modern account of Shetland is still a *desideratum*. All that is aimed at in the following pages, is to present a few truthful pictures of a wild and primitive district, and of a state of society rapidly disappearing under the influence of modern advancement. Shetland, as it still is, is not very different, in many important particulars, from what it was in the days of "Magnus Troil" of hospitable memory. But steam navigation, enterprize, and capital, are producing rapid changes here as elsewhere, so that "*passing away*" is written legibly on the dwellings—the fields and gardens—all, indeed, but the old rocks themselves.

We hail improvements—but we cling notwithstanding to early memories and ancient usages; and would gladly see them delineated on something less perishable than oral tradition, and especially in an abler style than we may hope to attain in the attempt.

The first thing that strikes a stranger on landing in Shetland, is the total absence of trees. Without doubt there have been woods here once; for decayed trunks are found in the bogs. They have probably been improvidently cut down, without leaving sufficient shelter for the young growth. But whether trees can now be raised, is a question which, though frequently proposed, is too often answered in the negative; thus taking for granted what has never been proved by any experiment conducted on a scale sufficiently enlarged, persevering, and intelligent. Some gentlemen have succeeded in rearing trees of respectable size in their gardens; and in Norway woods thrive in a latitude much farther north. Why not then in Shetland? Is the cause to be sought in intense cold, or long-continued frosts? Nay; for the temperature of these islands is more equable than in many other parts of Britain; and in a few well-sheltered valleys, the crops are as early ripe as in most districts of the North of Scotland. But there is one very peculiar and obvious reason that may account for the slow and imperfect growth, or total failure of any plantation of wood, hitherto attempted, which is, that the attenuated sea spray is, from the insular position of the land, carried over its whole surface by almost every storm that blows, and storms are frequent at all seasons of the year. After a high wind, especially from the west, when it has wreaked its fury on the wide Atlantic, every leaf and blade, together with the hair on the animals that browse on the commons, is impregnated with salt spray; so that vegetation is checked, and the green leaves blackened even at midsummer. Can it be wondered at, that the enthusiasm of the lovers of trees and flowers, is sorely tried, when one day they are exulting in the blossoms they have fostered and coaxed into beauty, and on the next, every petal and bud of hope is drooping and scorched, as if a

shrivelling fire had passed over it; and this is what
the Shetlanders are so often doomed to witness,
and from which even a high garden-wall is not
sufficient protection. Still, it is frequently said,
even this difficulty might be overcome; and as,
could woods, or even plantation belts, be made to
grow, the general fertility of the arable soil would
be increased,—besides the added beauty to the
landscape, we trust, amidst other improvements,
some Shetlanders will soon be found resolved to do
what can be done to wipe off, as it were, this reproach of barren poverty from their country.

But the great *general* defect in the Shetland climate, is the comparative absence of sun-shine, and
consequent want of regular and high temperature
in the summer months, inducing a heavy, damp
dulness, particularly trying to the mental, as well
as physical energies of all that are not natives, and
to many even of them. The cheering smiles of the
" god of day" are too often shrouded in low clouds,
and the face of nature obscured by surly fogs, even
in those months, when the sun is in his highest altitude, and we naturally expect genial warmth and
brightness. In winter, again, frost and snow are
much more rare than might be anticipated from the
latitude; but gales of wind, and heavy rains, are of
almost daily occurrence.

The geological formation of the Shetland Isles,
is mainly what is called *primitive;* and all the rocks
belonging to this formation are found here. Rooness Hill is of *granite;* and Unst, the most northerly island, has several hills of *serpentine*, in which is

found chromate of iron or, more properly, *chrome ore.* The first indications of this valuable mineral (which is used in arts and manufactures), were observed about forty years ago; but it was not till about 1823 that it was found in marketable quantity, by Thomas Edmonston, Esq. of Buness At first it realised £10 a ton; but for some years past its value has decreased to not above a fifth of that sum.

The botany of the country was surveyed some years ago, by a youthful and very talented native, and published in a work called " A Flora of Shetland." Several plants, mosses, and sea-weeds, not previously met with in Britain, are described as to be found in these islands.

In ornithology,—especially in the department of aquatic birds,—Shetland presents an inviting field to the lovers of that science. The sea and the shores indeed, teem with life ; so that every diversity of sound and motion there animates the solitude ; while the pleasure of unalloyed communion with nature, is enhanced by the consideration, that these scenes in Shetland are not inconveniently distant from the comforts and appliances of ordinary civilized life.

The domestic quadrupeds are all of diminutive size, and distinct breeds. Ponies, cattle, and pigs, as well as sheep, may be observed in a semi-savage state on the hills and commons all the year round.

In some of the islands mice are not found, and many of them are free from the still greater annoyance of rats, or any other ground vermin. Rabbits, however, are numerous, and hares have been introduced, but do not seem to increase so rapidly as was at first anticipated.

Shetland contains 33,000 inhabitants, scattered over the islands in hamlets and isolated dwellings. There is only one small town, with a population of 3000.

The land is generally low, sloping to the shore every where, with the exception of a few precipitous headlands of no great height. In the interior parts, bare hills and bleak moorlands,—the coarse herbage here and there cropped by some frightened-looking nondescript animals,—are all that greet the traveller's eye ; and occasionally he finds a little glen or valley, at the bottom of which reposes, in the most sequestered solitude, a very small fresh-water lake.

Along the banks of the bays and numerous friths or *voes*,* it is, that the soil is cultivated, and the population reside. Here and there, a tolerably large house, roofed with grey slate or flag-stone is seen, surrounded with numerous low farm-buildings or out-houses. These are the dwellings of the proprietors of the soil, between each of which miles generally intervene; while, on some of the islands,—and those generally the most fertile and prosperous,—there is no other gentleman's residence but the laird's, and it may be *the manse*. More thickly distributed, especially in localities

---

* *Voe*, an arm of the sea or *fiord*.

where the population clusters most, are a few second and third-rate houses, for the accommodation of the small shop, or rather store-keepers, vernacularly dignified into "*merchants;*" and where a little of every thing is kept for sale,—groceries and hardware,—bread-stuffs and clothing,—all reposing side by side in amicable arrangement.

The cottages of the tenantry are low, covered with turf, and then scantily thatched with oat-straw. They are divided into two apartments; the outer and larger one is used for all common family purposes; the fire-place, without a chimney, is near to one end, and several beds or sleeping-places, each enclosed like a cupboard, are at the other. These dormitories serve as a partition from a small panelled room, where the heads of the family repose, and which also serves as the especial guest-chamber; it has a window and chimney, but no grate. Peat being the only fuel used, burns much better and more cheerfully on the ample well swept hearth.

Shetland being, as we have stated, an archipelago, the inhabitants of each island,—though all united by various common interests, and many of them by still dearer ties,—are separated from each other, by a strait of the sea, more or less broad and hazardous. It is to be understood, therefore, that each man possesses at least a share of a *boat;* quite as necessary an appendage to him, as the horse to an Arab,—the rifle to a Backwoodsman,—or his tools to the mechanic. The boats are of all sizes, from eight to twenty feet in keel. The former are called

" whillies,"—the others are " four oared," or " six
oared." All are pointed at both ends, like the
Norwegian yawl; indeed, the keels and boards,
ready shaped, are frequently imported from Bergen
and Christiana. The six-oared boats have a mast,
and one large square-sail; but when wind is unsteady or contrary, they are propelled by the oars.
The circumjacent ocean, then, and intervening
sounds and ferries, may be seen constantly tra-
versed by these little vessels; and during the long
days and " dim obscure" night hours of the summer,
the sea is every where thickly dotted with those
engaged in fishing.

To see the multitude of those frail-looking skiffs,
with their large sails, like the wing of a butter-
fly,—the sun shining on *them*, long after the hull
becomes invisible,—disappearing one after another
on the measureless waters, as they wend their
way to the Haff, or deep-sea fishing,—is a touching, a most interesting sight; and is, or can be,
seldom witnessed without an inward breathing to
the Ruler of wind and waves, that these barks,
so preciously freighted with husbands, sons, and
fathers, may be preserved in peril, and conducted
back in safety.

CHAPTER II.

THE SHETLANDERS.

THERE is scarcely a spot in Shetland much above two miles distant from the sea, the larger islands being every where deeply indented with bays and *voes*, some of the latter of which run several miles inland. The dwellings, as mentioned in the last chapter, are always placed as close as possible to the water-side. Such being the topography, it will be readily imagined that the population is exclusively maritime. They are not indeed *amphibious*, like the seals and otters on their coasts, or like the nations of the lovely South Sea Islands. Strange to say, the Shetlanders, though expert sailors and industrious fishermen, very seldom bathe or learn to swim, though the latter acquirement would prove the means of saving many a valuable life, in the numerous accidents to which they are exposed. Yet still the Shetlandmen (with the exception of a very few masons and carpenters) all, as a matter of course, seek their livelihood on the bosom of the deep. Many of the young men enter the navy or merchant service, as seamen, and are found in every corner of the globe where British commerce has penetrated or British enterprize carried her ships. In his native place, also, the Shetlander is naturally, and from boyhood, a fisherman. He has indeed a few acres of land attached to his cottage, where he may cultivate potatoes, bear,* and oats, and feed two or three cows; but he pays his rent and provides most of the necessaries of life, by means of fishing; and, if to these bleak isles are denied genial climate and fertile soil, to clothe them with beauty, and cause the earth to pour forth food; yet the all bounteous Father of his creatures, compensates in a great measure for these deficiencies, by abundant supplies of fish of every kind. Though storms are frequent, they are generally of short duration, and it is not often that much longer time than a week elapses during which there is not some opportunity of fishing.

In the summer months, ling, tusk, and cod are caught for the purpose of being cured, to supply the British and Foreign markets. From May until August, the men are assembled at the different stations, where an overseer or factor is appointed to receive and superintend the salting and drying of the fish, either for the landlords, or for any company or individual that may have engaged in the undertaking. Huts of stone and turf are erected at the stations, where the men lodge when ashore; and it is only from Saturday evening till Monday morning that they are with their families. The household and little farm affairs are left to the care

---

* *Bear*, a coarse species of barley.

of the females, one of whom almost daily visits the station, from whence she carries home any inferior sort of fish that may be caught (halibut and skate chiefly), together with the *heads* of the ling and cod, for the family's present use.

The deep-sea, or "haff" fishing, is carried on chiefly through the night, or "the dim," as it is here called; for in this latitude there is at that season no darkness. The fishermen leave the shore in the afternoon, or earlier, according to the distance they may have to go to their usual fishing ground; they remain out till morning, or if the weather be very fine and settled, they are often absent two nights, from twenty to forty miles distant from land, in an open boat, and with no other refreshment than a jar of butter-milk-whey, and a cake of oatmeal.

The old men and boys, on the other hand, put off each fine evening in smaller skiffs, upon the bosom of the "voes" and bays, where, with a "hand-line," or a rude rod, and limpet-bait, they take the small fish with which these sheltered waters abound, viz. small rock cod, and the young of the coal-fish, which latter are called *sillacks* in their first year, and *piltacks* in the next two. These fish are from six to twelve inches long, and are very nutritious, wholesome, and even delicate eating when newly caught; but the Shetlanders prefer all fish after it has been slightly salted, and hung in the peat smoke till partially dried.

Fish, with oat-bread or potatoes, alas, in too many seasons of late, without any accompaniment

at all, forms the three daily meals of the Shetland
cottager. During winter, oatmeal porridge once
a-day may be enjoyed; and on rare holidays only,
bear broth, or a piece of pickled pork and cabbage.

The *coal-fish*, of which in ordinary seasons a
supply so bounteous is sent to every cottage door
in Shetland, have very large and fat livers; these
are used partly, when quite fresh, baked in the
oatmeal bread, or dressed with the fish instead of
butter; but by far the greater portion is suffered
to become rancid, and is then boiled down for *oil* to
feed the lamp that cheers the long winter evenings.
The livers, indeed, of all the fish that are caught,
are the perquisites of the men (not included in the
delivery of the fish to the factors), whereby considerable gain additional arises, besides supplying
their households with light.

Each cottage may also have *fuel* in abundance.
The peat moors are apportioned to the tenants,
along with their farms or crofts; and during the
months of June and July, the peats,—cut by the
men before the fishing season commences,—are
dried, and carried home on the backs of ponies, by
the industry of the young women and boys, and at
no other expense.

Among the lower class in Shetland, there are *two*
remnants of ancient usage, which we believe are
peculiar to these islands, at least in the British empire. The one is the use of the "old style" in
reckoning the days of the month, a practice which
they will not be persuaded to relinquish, though
they can give no reason whatever for its retention.

The other is, the custom of *patronymics*. Thus the children of James Johnson call themselves "James-sons," or "James-daughters;" those of Magnus Robertson are "Magnus-son," or more commonly, its abbreviation, "Manson." It was, as we all know, the same custom in the days of yore, that gave rise to the Jacksons, the Andersons, or the more courtly Fitz-Geralds and Fitz-Roys in England,—to the tribes of MacDonalds, &c. in Scotland; and to the O'Briens, &c. in Ireland. The Shetland seaman, however, is beginning to find it inconvenient, to bear in other countries a surname different from that of his father; and, therefore, of late, the families are more generally adopting their parent's name. The wives of the peasantry never assume their husbands', but retain their own maiden names. It is very common, especially in some of the districts, for individuals to acquire especial cognomens,—often amounting to nicknames,—either from the place of their birth or residence, or from some peculiar circumstance in their history, which they retain *nolens-volens*, to the complete oblivion of their family designation. But this is common in other parts of the North of Scotland also, and in Ireland.

A very general idea prevails in South Britain that the Gaelic is spoken in these islands, but this is quite a mistake. The two most distinct races of men, from which the British nation has sprung, are well known to be the Gael, and the Sassenach or Teuton. In Wales, in Ireland, and in the North and West of Scotland, we find obvious traces of the former, and of their language. But the *Gael* seems never to have inhabited Orkney and Shetland; which were perhaps *first*, and at all events, *finally* peopled by the genuine sons of the *Northmen*. Consequently the only remains of a peculiar tongue in these islands, are words and phrases of the *Norse*, a dialect of the language spoken in Iceland and Norway, and immortalized in the Scandinavian Sagas.

The Shetland vernacular is now good English, intermixed, amongst the peasantry, with peculiar names and words, which it would puzzle a Highlander, but not a Dane to understand. The gentry, it is allowed, speak extremely well. Their pronunciation bears a much nearer resemblance to the educated Irish than to the Scotch; and it would seem their organs of speech are peculiarly flexible, and their ear good; as foreigners remark, they acquire other languages in great purity. The tone of voice of the Shetlanders generally is soft, and pitched in a rather plaintive key.

There are twelve parish clergymen of the Established Church of Scotland, assisted in a few instances by missionaries on the Church Extension Schemes. A small number of persons profess other creeds, as Methodists and Dissenters from the Establishment; but there are no Roman Catholics.

In many of the parishes, which have a radius of seven to twelve miles, or where a stormy tideway rolls between the several districts, or different islands of which such parishes are composed, there are two or three churches, in which it is the minister's duty to officiate. This he can accomplish only on successive Sabbaths in turn. Fair-Isle and Foula have a visit from him only *once a-year!*

In all the parishes, there is a school attached to the Established Church, as in the other districts of Scotland ; but there are supplementary schools under the superintendance of other educational committees, so that there are now, it is understood, hardly any grown persons throughout the islands, who cannot read; and the generation now springing up very generally acquire writing. The latter is an art so obviously invaluable to the absent and their friends, that the poor Shetlanders often make considerable sacrifices to attain it.

Inquisitiveness, it is generally observed, is a marked characteristic of the Shetlander; and when under the guidance of principle and good feeling, of course it leads to the acquirement of much valuable information by those who have opportunity. Hence our islanders when absent from their fatherland, are invariably remarked as extremely intelligent. At home, however, this same trait too often degenerates into passion for gossip, hunting out private history, and finally into the most reckless slander.

It must, on the whole, be admitted, they are by no means a religious people. They seem to be totally deficient in that deep, reverential impression of sacred things, which has so long, and so favourably distinguished the Scottish peasantry. Though almost universally sober, and decorous in their demeanour, it is a general matter of com-

plaint by their religious instructors, that they do
not appear to be actuated by the principles, or animated by the sentiments, of the blessed faith they
profess.   On the one hand, overt crimes of serious
magnitude are very rare.   We leave the outward
doors of our dwellings during the whole year without lock or bar; we allow linens to remain out all
night to bleach or dry in perfect security, and have
never to mourn over such revolting acts of cruelty
and recklessness, as every now and then disgrace
the cities and even villages of England.   On the
other hand, truth for the most part is utterly disregarded,—even the sacred sanction of an oath in
evidence has not its proper weight in inducing
adherence to verity; the passion for gossip begets
and fosters habits of evil speaking and suspicion;
and the practice of secret pilfering prevails to a
great extent.   And, further, let the reader observe
with commiseration, how this lamentable deficiency
of pious feeling acts upon the happiness of these
interesting islanders.   From their manner of life
they are constantly exposed to the most deplora-
ble accidents.   Where then are the consolations
that might soften to survivors unexpected and
overwhelming bereavements?   Possessed naturally
of susceptible and acute feelings, where is the
guardian spirit that would still the torturing throb
of anxiety and suspense?   Where the soothing
balm for the wound of sad and sudden separations?
A storm overtakes the fishers, when many miles
distant from land, and from the too common custom of members of one household forming the crew

of the same boat, we often witness the pitiable case, of a wretched female losing, at a stroke, husband, sons, and brothers,—and youthful widows left to mourn the short period of wedded happiness they had enjoyed,—while numerous helpless children are thrown on the charity of the neighbourhood,—a charity, by the way, never appealed to in vain. In these, and similar cases, long and bitterly do survivors mourn. Months elapse ere they enter any other dwelling, or even present themselves in the house of God; their loss is never alluded to, even after distance of time, without floods of tears, and the names of those they deplore never escape their lips. However long the span of life that may be allotted to her, the young widow *never* lays aside the badge of her desolate state,—"the garments of her widowhood,"—except in the rare cases where she makes a second choice, and even then, her apparel is plain and sad-coloured, her demeanour chastened and subdued,—she never seems to forget for a moment that she has been a "widow and desolate." Should she have a pledge of her early love, or a child by another husband, she gives it the name of him she lost, though she will always find a pet name by which to compromise the once familiar appellative; and she will cling with redoubled, and distinguishing fondness to this second precious one, perhaps, if a son, only to lose him in like manner, and to mourn over him with more intense and inconsolable sorrow. This is no overstrained or imaginary description, but only what is familiar to every one in the least acquainted with the cha-

racter and position of the Shetland cottars. Were
the hearts thus too often shrouded in the darkness
of affliction, more open to the holy light of religion,—were its impressions more permanent,—its
influence more exerted on the conduct and occur-
rences of every-day life,—would not even the lamentable dispensations we have referred to, be more
composedly, more hopefully borne; and the everlasting consolations of the gospel shine steadily
through the thickest clouds of adversity. We have
dwelt the more particularly on this point because
we consider it the great,—the cardinal defect in
the Shetland character; and because closely connected with it, is another trait, most influential
on the people's habits and happiness. We al-
lude to the firm and universal hold, that various
forms of *superstition* retain on their belief and
practice.

By far the most distressing of these is that
which is connected with deceased friends,—re-ap-
pearances and dreams of whom they as invariably
expect, as they shrink from. A vague mysterious
fear invests the departed, even those who have
been nearest and dearest, and especially in the case
of the drowned. When a death occurs in a neighbourhood, all sorts of omens and warnings are recollected and recounted, till no person will go a
step, or remain alone, on any consideration; the
men being quite as much victimized as the females
under this ignorant, supernatural terror. Should
a boat be lost at sea, as is so often the case, the
unquiet ghosts are believed to be wandering about

all their accustomed places of resort, and will by
no means be at rest, unless spoken to, *which is
never done!* or unless the bodies are cast ashore,
and receive Christian sepulture,—or until, finally,
the fishes and other denizens of the sea, have
caused all vestiges of the mortal remains to be in-
tangible. The name of a person deceased must
never be uttered, else on the first favouring opportunity, the ghost will stand before the incautious
speaker, as if he had been called; and, therefore, if
it becomes necessary to converse about any such
departed one, he is designated by his late abode or
parentage, or any-how, *except* by his own proper
appellation. Some old houses,—many lonely spots
among the hills, and certain deep gullies and peat-
moors, are understood to be *haunted*, in consequence
of their connection with some hidden crime or
other, existing only in some wild legends, or as wild
modern imaginings.

This belief in apparitions is indeed current in
most communities, and perhaps, it is a safer, as well
as a more natural thing, than the denial of all faith
in spiritual influences. But certainly we have not
heard of its being *practically* carried to so great
lengths any where as among the Shetland peasantry. No amount of argument or example makes
the slightest impression; they cling to their early
imbibed opinions as to the faith of their fathers;
and should one imagine he has succeeded in con-
vincing their reason to the contrary, the very first
opportunity that presents itself will prove how
much he is mistaken, if he expected that *reason*

would control the early perverted powers of imagination.

Another of the universal superstitions of the
Shetlanders, is that relating to the Drougs or
Trows; in the present day more generally called
"*Fairy Folk.*" But these are essentially a different race from the classical subjects of Oberon,
who people the flower-bells,—drink from acorn
cups,—and float on the moon-beams; and from
the Irish fairies that dance round the daisies, and
feast under the mushroom; and even from the
useful and good-natured Scottish *brownie.* The
Shetland Trow lives under ground,—is nearly of
human size, or at least may adopt this form at
pleasure,—is always clad in sober gray, and likes
to interfere in human affairs,—particularly desiring
to have earth-born nurses and infants, or a fair
bride for one of their princes, now and then! The
Shetlander, however, carefully eschews these fa-
vours; and that more especially, as mere malice is
understood often to actuate the Trow in his tricks.
In the instances of brides,—peculiarly fine or
beautiful children,—and child-bed women, sundry
charms are invariably employed to guard against
the designs of these intermeddling "folk." Sticks
laid in the form of a cross at the chamber-door,—
a knife placed on the bed in a peculiar position;
but above all, a Bible or Testament beneath the
pillow, or in the baby's cradle, is *never omitted.*
If a child, which has been fair and thriving, becomes wan and shrivelled, or weak from disease
or defective nourishment, it is at once imagined

that it has been *exchanged* through some neglect
of the above precautions on the mother's part. In
cases when health is restored, the credit of the
cure is given to the *power* certain persons are
supposed to possess, who, by peculiar charms,
compel the "fairy folk" to restore their victim.
The wildest and most extraordinary legends are
then related, of all the earth-born saw and experienced during his sojourn with these *sub-earthly*
beings,—a period sometimes amounting to several
years ! These are not, be it observed, " old wives
stories" to frighten or amuse children, such as are
to be found in the traditionary lore of many country people besides the Shetlanders. With the
latter they are the current absurdities of the day
that is passing, and the knowes (or knolls) underneath which these "good people" congregate,—
the solitary springs whence they fetch water,—and
the especial evenings on which they busy themselves in mundane matters, are all heedfully noted,
and at any other risk avoided.

The belief in *witchcraft*, nearly exploded elsewhere, yet lingers in Shetland. Certain persons
are supposed to possess *hereditarily* this power
from the evil one ; which, however, is not so often
exercised as it might be, especially if they are duly
propitiated, and cause of offence avoided, which,
it is almost needless to say, is carefully attended
to. Such individuals may rob of its richness or
" profit" their neighbour's dairy, or blast with
their curse the person or effects of one who offends
them,—or even raise, like " Norna of Fitful

Head," the sudden squall or hurricane; and anon command it to peace by their spells. It is but a few years ago, that the writer lived in the house, with a young female servant, who was supposed to possess this dreaded power of witchcraft; and despite many remonstrances, she persisted in encouraging the delusion! On being found fault with one day for her mode of churning, she was observed to mutter a good deal, under the influence of habitual irritation of temper, and *no butter came that day!* Of course the culprit had put a bit of alum into the churn, but her fellow-servants, and others, were persuaded a very different cause was to blame. About the same time, it happened that a newly married young woman was seized with paralysis of her limbs. The husband applied for no medical assistance, but went to all the "wise women" within reach for advice, if haply some one of them might at least assign a cause for, or point out the author of, his wife's affliction. At length a person, who it may be supposed, had discovered some particulars of his private history, suggested that he had paid his addresses to the servant girl above mentioned, which further enquiry confirmed; as also the fact, that she had been heard to threaten the person who supplanted her in his affections with mysterious vengeance. Will it be believed, that the unfortunate young husband actually came to the supposed originator of his calamity, to beseech her pity on his poor wife! After a pretty long conference, the *soi-disant* witch permitted him to prick her arm, and carry with him a drop or two of the blood from her vein, to apply to the palsied limbs. This strange interview, which several persons witnessed, though the discourse was not overheard, and its terms were never known, was conducted with the most serious gravity and decorum, and they shook hands at parting. But the wife did not recover. The husband, after her death, left the country, to which he never returned,—ever believing his wife had been " witched." And the witch still lives,— ugly it must be owned, and sullen,—still in the prime of life, and having the same ill repute as before.

Among a variety of superstitious practices, less objectionable than those we have mentioned, though equally devoid of piety and common sense, we shall only notice the following, which, so far as we know, is peculiar to one or two of the Shetland islands, but is common in the remoter glens of Norway. When a child is not thriving, or is affected by some unknown malady, and yet has not any peculiar *look* to stamp it as " fairy striken ;" or rather, perhaps, when the parents are willing to believe any other harm than *that* has befallen their child, the mother goes round to all her acquaintances, especially to those, if she has any, among the gentry, " to beg nine women's meat" for the little sufferer. This is a plea never refused ; and the mother is presented with three different kinds of eatables, from nine mothers, who have no unhealthy children. These things are carefully set aside, and the patient scrupulously fed with them, and with nothing else, till they are finished. It will be easily credited that a variety of nourishing articles of diet will be often most beneficial to a poor child, who has too likely suffered from defective, or un-wholesome food; but the mother and others will tell you, the cure lay in the especial charm; and should it fail, several very sufficient reasons will be suggested,—as want of faith in some of the donors,—a part of the *medicine* having been ab-stracted by others for whom it was not intended, &c., &c.

Many unreasonable and groundless superstitions, connected with the sea and the fishing, are also practised exclusively by the men. But sea-faring people, we know, are proverbially given to credu-lity, and therefore we must not be too hard on the Shetlanders, for what many others better instruct-ed are equally blame-worthy.

CHAPTER III.

TOPOGRAPHICAL SKETCH OF THE ISLANDS.

SHETLAND lies between 59° and 61° north latitude. The islands cluster in a compact group, two or three of them only lying above four miles distant from the others. There are above a hundred in all, thirty of which are inhabited; the rest being appropriated to grazing. Every isolated rock, whose summit, of a few roods square, is spread with a scanty verdure, feeds a sheep or two. Such solitary and often elevated pasture-grounds are vernacularly termed *holms* and *skerries*. These designations, and also the names of most of the places, are derived from the Norse, or original language of Scandinavia, of which Shetland was for centuries an integral portion.

The largest island round which (except on the south) the rest group, is called

MAINLAND.

IT is sixty miles long, but of very irregular breadth; in some places it is ten or twelve miles across; and in one part it seems as if the wild Atlantic waves would soon form a permanent barrier between two of its districts, there being only a neck of land, not a hundred yards over, between sea and sea. This singular isthmus is called *Mavis-grind;* * and a wilder spot one need not desire to meet with, especially on a stormy winter's day. *North Mavin* is the name of the northern district of Mainland separated from the rest by Mavis-grind. It is the most romantic part of Shetland, though perhaps least visited by strangers because of its remote position. Its western shore is exposed to the full force of the broad Atlantic surges; consequently the rocks lie scattered, for the distance of perhaps a mile from the land, in the greatest variety of size and shape it is possible to conceive, besides hellyers† and arches innumerable. It is as if one gazed on the ruins a mighty flood had left, of what may have been temples and pinnacles and gorgeous monuments of art; and the mind is intensely affected by the idea of what must be the power of those winds and waves that toss about such gigantic fragments, easily as a child flings its pebbles here and there on the strand.

To the seal-hunter and ornithologist also, these holms and hellyers present an inviting field of exploration. On a calm day, under a bright sun, or the summer's soft twilight, the scene is very grand,—imposing in its vastness and perfect repose; and we imagine that a visit to North Mavin cannot but prove a treat to the tourist, fatigued

---

* *Grind*, a gate or gateway.
† *Hellyer*, a low-roofed dark cavern.

with the glare of cities, or the dull routine of commonly frequented watering-places, more especially so, if he is desirous to study the touching lesson, how puny an architect man is in comparison with his Maker.

Rooness Hill is another attractive feature in this part of Shetland. It is a huge granite mass, the highest land in the islands, being of the altitude of 1500 feet. It is steep and rugged on the west side, but on the south-east it may be easily ascended. From the summit the whole Archipelago may be viewed as in a map,—islands large and small, with their narrow creeks and friths, and snug sheltered bays, while encircling all, is Britain's glorious bulwark—the sea.

The southern promontory of Mainland and of Shetland is called *Dunrossness*.* The terminating cape is *Sumburgh Head*, on which is a light-house. A little to the north-westward of this is *Fitful Head*, the world-renowned residence of the Reim Kennar, *Norna*. Dunrossness is the best cultivated, and most fertile parish of Shetland ; and to those in search of the picturesque, affords some pleasing and romantic rides.

Until within the last few years there were no roads whatever in Shetland ; the traveller had to be content to traverse bare hills, boggy plains, and sheep worn pathways ; but since 1848, when the potato failure caused so much destitution, good roads have been made, for constructing which, the

---

* *Ness* in all cases means a point of land or promontory.

people were paid in meal and seed-corn and potatoes ; and thus what seemed an unmixed evil, has
resulted in an undoubted good. A trunk line of
road traverses the length of Mainland and of Yell,
while shorter cuts branch off to a few of the more
populous districts elsewhere.

Scalloway is a village, or perhaps embryo town,
on the west side of Mainland, distant about five
miles from *Lerwick* the metropolis, or rather the
only town as yet in the country. The ride across
is a much frequented one ; the scenery is very pleasing, and there is a ruinous castle at Scalloway,
built in 1600 by Earl Patrick Stuart, a rather un-
scrupulous governor in those days.

Bressa Sound, forming the harbour and road-
stead of Lerwick, is a spacious basin or bay, across
the bosom of which stretches the island of Bressa,
leaving a narrow entrance-channel to the north and
south.

Approaching Lerwick from the south, will be
seen numerous low points of land on the left, or
Mainland coast, and on Bressa, wave-worn cliffs of
sandstone, slate, and high bluff headlands, forming
together a picturesque and graceful entrance to
the port. A few miles before reaching this " south
entry," the visitor will be called to observe a low
island named MOOSSA, to which in all probability
he will afterwards make a forenoon's excursion, as
it contains the most perfect specimen of those singular structures called *Pictish Burghs*, now to be
found in Britain, though less complete examples
are numerous on the islets and seaward points and

headlands of Shetland. That these burghs, which consist of masses of stone-work, without doors or windows, were beacon-towers or strong-holds of the renowned Scandinavian rovers who peopled these islands soon after the Christian era began, is the theory Shetlanders generally prefer, to that which has stamped them as of Pictish origin. But as antiquarian authorities are at issue on the point, we only state deferentially our own opinion, leaving wiser heads to decide the point, or still contest it, as the case may be. At all events a visit to Moossa will amply repay the time and trouble to those curious in such things.

BRESSA.

ON the south-west of the island of Bressa, as was previously indicated, there rises frowningly a precipitous cliff, which, at the base, is broken (as in other similar localities) into many a wild geo* and shattered crevice, where no foot save that of sea-fowl ever rested, guarded as they are by the terrific power of the giant, " Old Ocean." Near the point are two stupendous pillars, arched overhead, beneath which said giant roars and rages incessantly, the noise of his howling before and after a south-east gale being heard at many miles distance. A little farther, on the same side, is a singularly beautiful cave, not so well known as it deserves to be, because of the difficulty of approaching it, except in the finest and most settled weather.

---

* *Geo*—pronounced with *g* hard, as *gyo*—a small creek.

A magnificent arch forms a vestibule, the roof and walls of which are adorned with brilliant colouring of every hue. Turning to the right is a long tortuous cavern, which can only be seen by the aid of torches, so completely is daylight excluded from its winding recesses. The roof is lofty, the sides are composed of magnificent stalactites, which look as if carved by a cunning workman into every possible device. Gigantic figures in priestly cowls, and with folded hands,—cherubim with outstretched wing,—and monstrous Nineveh-like animals of every size are there. Imagination, at least, would fain assign, as we linger, a thousand names to forms chiselled by no mortal hand, but displaying to the admirer of Nature's designs, another most interesting specimen of the workmanship of its Author. " The Orkneyman's Cave," as this romantic spot is called, winds inwards, till it becomes too narrow for a boat to proceed ; but as all sounds, instead of returning in echoes, reverberate and die away in long " hollow murmurs," we infer, that at some considerably distant point there is an opening or outlet to the upper air again. The place acquired its name from the following circumstance :—

A seaman, a native of Orkney, being chased by a press-gang, took refuge on a squally day under the gigantic archway, where his pursuers dared not follow him. His empty boat being afterwards found, his friends believed he had perished, braving death in the boiling surges, rather than be dragged from his home, and a sweet Shetland maiden, his

betrothed bride. Meanwhile the hunted sailor had
ventured into the inner cave, and found a hiding-
place on a ledge or table of rock in its darkest recesses. Patiently—bravely—he rested two days,
in his wild, yea terrible abode; and say, did the
booming, almost deafening thunder of the sea talk
to him of life, and hope, and love, during this tremendous probation? Perhaps it did. At all
events, the Providence in whom we hope he put his
trust, willed it so, that a calmer day permitted him
to swim to the base of a portion of the cliff outside, which he scaled, and obtained rest and food
in the nearest cottage. The kindly inmates hid
him till the departure of the hated press-gang,
when he was restored to his friends, and united to
the object of his affections.

A couple of miles walk across Bressa, conducts
to the little island of

NOSS,

WHICH forms a fertile pasture-farm, and and has a
precipice which rises about 700 feet above the sea.
Nearly on a level with a less elevated part of the
cliff, is a detached rock, called " *The Holm of Noss*."
It is precipitous on all sides, but on the top is food
enough for six or eight sheep. How to get there
was the query? An adventurous cragsman at
length climbed from a boat to the top of the holm,
where he fixed some strong stakes in the ground,
over which was passed a thick cable. On this was
slung a " cradle," or box, in which one person pulls
himself, or is pulled across by ropes and pulleys.

The tremulous motion,—the terrific gulf,—and above all, the stepping into and out of the cradle, render this aërial voyage too trying for the nerves of most people, though many visitors make a point of accomplishing it,—and *cui bono?* We confess ourselves not to have arrived at that pitch of romance, which understands terror to be a necessary or desirable ingredient in the idea of the sublime; and though no accident has hitherto occurred, we would much rather read a slight description of this far-famed " cradle of Noss," than attempt a transit in it, or even look on while others more adventurous undertake it.

LERWICK.

EXACTLY opposite the west side of Bressa is Lerwick, the most northerly town in the British Isles. Its situation is extremely good. The spacious bay is completely land-locked, the land curves gracefully, and the shores slope gradually to the water's edge. The town is built on the slope, and some good houses crown the heights. Consequently the cross streets, or rather lanes, are steep as well as narrow, while one main street winds as the shore winds, and is bordered with shops and dwellings, in every possible position; the only invariable rule appearing to be, that no two are alike, or any one set in a line even with its neighbour. As there are few vehicles, the chief thorough-fares are paved with flag-stones, while several small quays with steps lead to the sea, which is so deep, that some good houses and warehouses have their foundation, and have even one storey of the building, beneath low water.

There are four places of worship, viz. the Parish Church, and one each for congregations of the Free Kirk,—United Presbyterians,—and Wesleyan Methodists.

The society in Lerwick is very circumscribed. There are but a few families of the native gentry of the country. The rest of the inhabitants, besides the erratic class of seamen, are thriving and respectable shopkeepers and small tradesmen. In the houses of the first mentioned, will be found much of the polish, and all the comforts of residences in what might be imagined more *civilized*, because more southern latitudes! As hospitality is here frankly and unsparingly practised, there is no public inn, and strangers are invariably favourably impressed with the unpretending and gracious kindness they receive. There are, however, one or two quiet and respectable lodging-houses.

It is often remarked, that in the article of dress alone, are the Lerwegians rather incongruous. They are decidedly partial to display in this particular; so that it has been said, the costume of the ladies is more adapted to Edinburgh promenades, than to a remote and not very bright or cleanly little sea-port.

There are no public buildings, except the churches, and no opportunity of public amusements. The residents in Lerwick, therefore, cultivate and enjoy their own domestic circle, and the small social group they may draw around their

hearths occasionally, and always the same individuals.   The only variety that presents itself, is the
arrival sometimes of foreign ships, and perchance
some of our own noble navy or merchantmen;
under which circumstances, the usually isolated
Shetlanders have opportunity of forming valuable
and lasting friendships.

During the last war there was a garrison of
about 200 veterans, with fourteen guns, in the
small fort built on a slight elevation on the north
side of the town. The situation commands the
harbour, but would be powerless to protect the
town were a hostile force to land (which may
Heaven forfend!) on some more southerly part of
the coast   Fort-Charlotte, after having been abandoned and dismantled for forty years, is now again
to be garrisoned and armed. As a mark of cour-
tesy and respect to the lonely isles which supply
many a brave seaman to our Royal and Commercial Navies, the measure is, we understand, a welcome one; but we more than suspect, our " poverty obscure," and, chiefly, the " wooden walls of
Old England," will prove, under Providence, the
Shetlanders' best defences in the day of war.

One other spot near Lerwick merits a short
notice, because of an anecdote with which it is
connected.   In the bay, about two-thirds across to
Bressa, is a low rocky islet, called the " Holm of
Crooster."   It is about fifty yards in circumference,
and the sea-gull and cormorant are its only denizens. Fifty or sixty years ago, smuggling was
carried on to a considerable extent in these islands,

and the *Magnus Troils* and *Eric Icambesters* of those days, kept up a pretty brisk contraband traffic with Holland, and other places.

One dark winter night a boat was speeding from a small Dutch vessel in the harbour, to the opposite shore of Bressa, with a valuable cargo to be deposited in a snug hole of a lonely *geo*. A King's cutter in the "Preventive Service" had, however, unexpectedly stolen into Bressa Sound soon after dark, and the smuggling boat was warily pursued by one from the cutter, manned with a well-armed crew. The Lerwegian contrabandists were overtaken and captured; but on returning to Lerwick, a violent squall came on, and the prisoners proposed to their victors, that they should all take refuge on the Holm of Crooster. The night was dark as pitch, thick with drizzling drifting rain. The place was utterly strange to the "Preventive men," and they felt obliged to agree to the smugglers' proposal to land on the islet, where a safe shelter was assured to them. No sooner had the whole party stepped on the rock,—the prisoners civil and submissive to their apparently inevitable fate, than the latter, one by one, quickly returned to their boat, and cutting the other adrift, it was soon riding on the troubled waves and tide, far away in the German Ocean. They then bravely faced the increasing storm, and leaving the King's officer and men on the bare and desolate *holm*, landed and hid their cargo, and escaped to a distant island for the time. The helpless sojourners on the rock were next day relieved from their wet and comfortless quarters, not a little ashamed, it may well be supposed, of their share in the night's adventure.

THE NORTH ISLES.

PROCEED we now from Lerwick to visit " The North Isles." This may be accomplished by sea in an open boat, if the weather be very fine, or in one of the small sloops that weekly make an erratic voyage, with a few passengers, and a collection of goods as multifarious as are the wants of civilized life, to be landed at every port on the passage. Even bakers and butchers' supplies are only thus available to the North Isles people! But we may get north even more pleasantly, and not too fatiguingly, by the land way. A strong nimble pony carries the traveller through the parishes of Whiteness and Weesdale,—the road every now and then commanding a view of the numerous voes on the east side of Mainland, until we reach Mossbank, which is separated by a four miles strait or sound from the Island of Yell. By this route the North Isles postman travels on foot, " news from all nations lumbering on his back." A well manned boat ferries the traveller over a dangerous tide-way, at all seasons, even during very rough weather; but the boat is admirable,—the men brave, skilful, and experienced, so that accidents very rarely occur. We are now in

YELL,

WHICH is an oblong island, chiefly composed of peat-moors, so that its aspect is dark and bleak.

The new road here leads over many a chasm and
bog, smoothing the wanderer's path in a degree not
easily appreciated, except by the natives, who so
long floundered helplessly over moors and quag-
mires.   On the north and north-west of Yell,
the scenery is very wild, and one or two gentlemen's residences are the most retired, and even desolate in the country.   The hills and moors of
Yell feed great numbers of the diminutive sheep,
whose fleeces are of the peculiarly soft and silky
texture that makes Shetland hosiery so much
esteemed.

On the east of Yell, and about equi-distant from
it and Unst, lies

FETLAR,

A triangular island, containing about 500 fishermen, the laird's mansion, the church and the
manse.

Near to the eastern extremity of the island there
is a singular archway, through which the sea rushes
like a subterraneous river or canal, under a considerable space of pasture-ground, boiling and surg-
ing during winter in a most terrific fashion; even
in summer we are ignorant if any one has had
nerve enough to attempt this styx-like passage.

Between the north-east of Yell, and the south-
west of

UNST,

ROLLS a strong tide-way, about a mile broad.
Here again the traveller is ferried across, and

finds himself in the most northerly island of Shetland.

It is very different in appearance from most of the others, and much more densely peopled. Its hills are of gneiss and serpentine,—its hamlets pretty thickly scattered,—its fields, though small in extent, tolerably well cultivated; but chiefly here are to be seen a considerable number of slate-roofed dwellings, where lairds reside on their paternal properties, or shop-keepers, clergymen, and schoolmasters, pursue their several callings. Besides the excellent parish church, there are two " Free Kirks " and a Methodist Chapel, five school-houses, and above twenty-four shops. The whole population is about 3000.

Unst is considered the *Bath* or *Brighton* of Shetland. Trade, and a few of the *sober gaities* of country life are more cultivated here than elsewhere in Shetland, and for all this the people are, in a great measure, indebted to the mines of chrome ore worked in the island.

The north point of Unst is, like some of the other localities we have noted, grand in rock scenery. Here again are *hellyers, geos, holms,* and *skerries* in great variety and abundance. About a mile beyond the most northerly point are three or four naked rocks. On the highest there has been lately erected a light-house, the want of which has been long complained of by mariners.

When the tourist has thus visited the most hyperborean extremity in our gracious Queen's dominions, he will probably, on some fine day, take a marine excursion in one of the six-oared fishing-boats, to the wild and solitary " *Skerries*," about twenty-four miles from Unst, and the same distance from Lerwick. There are only a few fishermen's families resident here ; but as the islets are three or four in number, there is good pasturage on those that are uninhabited, and an extensive fishing-station. A beautiful revolving light has been recently placed here also; and the only harbour, in its closeness, security, and narrowness of entrance, has been observed to be the counterpart of that of Balaklava, lately the centre of so much intense and thrilling interest.

It only remains that we slightly notice other two outlying isles belonging to Shetland.

FOULA AND FAIR ISLE.

The former is situated about sixteen miles due west of Mainland. It is very high and quite precipitous, forming an extraordinary and most interesting feature in the view from Rooness Hill, or some other eminence in North Mavin. The cliffs of Foula are tenanted by innumerable sea-fowl, which prove a source of considerable profit to the remote inhabitants.

Fair Isle is above thirty miles to the south-west of Shetland, and contains about a hundred inhabitants, who obtain a livelihood by fishing and knitting. The former can be attempted only during a few weeks of the summer season, therefore the Fair Isle *men* do not disdain to knit as well as the women. The productions of both are a pecu-

liar quality of plain close knitting.   Caps, gloves,
and waistcoats are woven by these self-taught but
expert artists, with the most fantastic figures, and
great variety of colours, all dyed by themselves,
chiefly with herbs and lichens of native growth.
Thus do these solitary islanders beguile the loneli-
ness of their winter months, by brisk and in-
genious industry, the only kind indeed within their
reach; but from the remoteness of their locality,
not so remunerative as it ought to be.

CHAPTER IV.

THE SILLACK.

THE small fish called *sillack* and *piltack*, which so largely enters into the diet of the Shetland peasantry, is brought to their very doors by the waters of every bay and creek, so that even the aged females and children, may in moderate weather obtain a supply each morning and evening throughout the year. It is the young fry of a species of the *cod genus*, called, when full-grown, *saithe* or *coal-fish* (Gadus Carbonarius). In this latter state the fish is larger, coarser and darker coloured than the ling or cod; but until its third year, it is very delicate, as well as nourishing. In size and shape, and in liveliness and energy of motion, the saithe in all its stages of growth, strongly resembles the salmon. It is of a deep dark blue on the back, and the scales are large and strong.

A few further particulars of this, to a Shetlander all-important article of his *commissariat*, may not be uninteresting; the more especially as the fish seems to be confined in its *habitat*, to these northern latitudes. Occasionally it is caught in other parts of Scotland, and known there by the name of "*podley;*" but its native haunts appear to be the coasts of Caithness, Orkney and Shetland, Faroe and Norway.

In Shetland, when the month of May arrives, with its promise and its brightness, the first question every one asks his neighbour, is of the appearance of sillack. It is then very small, not above four inches in length, and is caught with the rod, morning and evening, chiefly in the tideways.

As summer advances, when the men are all engaged in the more important deep sea, or "haff" fishing, the sillacks are growing apace. The old men and boys,—too old or too young for " rowing to the haff," may be seen in their little "whilly" boats, during the long twilight, while females and others of the boys, without leaving the shore, wield their light rods over the crags, where the sillacks "most do congregate" in shoals, where the water is moderately deep, and when the weather is fine. As the fish are so small, however, and at that season shy, more than a few score may hardly be procured at a time. The *gude-wife* has ready a pot of boiling *sea water*, into which the sillacks, immediately on being brought ashore and gutted, are plunged, and after being boiled about five minutes, a delicious wholesome supper is before the waiting family. We believe, by-the-by, it is this early necessity of sitting up

till the hour of sillack fishing is past, that makes
the Shetland cottar habitually dislike "early to
bed and early to rise,"—the contrary being his
usual custom.

When the summer and autumn "white fishing"
is past, the stalwart men bend themselves to their
home harvest of the sea. In October, the sillacks
are in perfection, and are caught in the bays
in great numbers. This fishing is then very
amusing and successful sport. A boat commonly
contains three or four men, one of whom keeps
it steady by means of a pair of oars, or moves
it from place to place. The fishers are provided
with two, and often three or four rods, to which
are attached short lines of gut. There are three
or four hooks to each line,—the hooks being
nothing but *bent pins*, trimmed with an artificial
fly, home made. By this time, we mean in October, last year's *sillacks* have become *piltacks*, and
are caught at the same time, in a similar, though
not identical manner. The fishers put off in the
afternoon, and with the fly, first fish for sillacks ;
as soon as it becomes nearly dark they adopt the
regular hook, baited with parboiled limpits, and
draw piltacks.

The best place is just on the edge of the tide-
way, in the sounds, at the entrance of the several
bays. In favourable weather, and when the fish
are very plentiful, a man may draw in an evening
two bushels of sillacks. The largest number of
piltacks we remember to have heard counted, was

taken by a young gentleman one Saturday evening, between seven and ten o'clock; with three rods
he caught *nine hundred!* In the month of May
again, it is, that the sillacks *begin* to be called piltacks. A "May piltack" is a luxury fit for any
gentleman's table.

When the fisherman has more sillacks and piltacks than his family can use fresh, they are
banded together in pairs, dipped in salt and water,
and hung over a straw rope, either on the rafters
of the cottage, or on the gable ends outside. It is
very cheerful and *plentiful looking* to see the ends
of the lowly dwelling festooned in draperies of this
wholesome and palatable food. During some of
the late dismal seasons of failure of the potato
and oat crops, famine to a frightful extent must
have ensued, but for the providential abundance
of sillacks and piltacks. To be sure, many a delicate female, and hungry little babe, at times turned
almost with loathing from fish, without any addition of bread or potatoes, and many times the
weather was so stormy, that in their greatest
need the men could not put off a boat; but on the
whole, these islanders were chiefly, by means of
this food, preserved from much of the suffering
other destitute districts underwent. Even in seasons of ordinary productiveness from the land,
when a few days,—perchance a week or two
elapses, without fish in a Shetland cottage, the
family long for it, as for the most acceptable
treat, of which they may partake without stint.

At the *Foys*,* when the month of August ends,
the time-honoured toast still is—" The Lord open
the mouths of the grey fish,† and hold his hand
about our corn." Only on Christmas-day, or at
a wedding, are sillacks and piltacks inadmissible
on a Shetland cottar's table.

Will the reader now contemplate for a few
moments, another interesting and cheerful scene,
presenting a somewhat different phase of the sillack fishery. A small French vessel engaged in
the cod-fishing, on the shores of Iceland, had received some damage during a storm on her homeward voyage, and was with difficulty kept afloat
till she reached these islands, when her master put
into one of the Shetland bays, and by the pilot's
advice, ran her ashore on a sandy bank, where at
low tide she could lie nearly dry, and her cargo
therefore be taken out and partially saved. This
was done accordingly; but the vessel being found
unfit for repairs, was abandoned. Some of the
cargo of salted cod remained in the hold, or was
dropped in the landing. It was unusual, and
melancholy to see that vessel lying on her side,
the winter storms sweeping over her hull and pro-
strate masts. But what was the consequence?
February came, and an enormous shoal of sillacks

---

* Foy is a feast of gladness by the fishermen, their wives and
families (each boat's crew together) on the happy conclusion of
their summer's labours on the deep.

† *Grey fish*,—the saithe, as contra-distinguished from the ling
and cod, or "*white fish*."

was found around and within the hull of the
wreck, attracted thither by the dead cod. A
low stone-pier stretched nearly to the vessel, and
myriads of these small fish were seen in the clear
water, surrounding the pier at the flood-tide.
They all lay with their heads in one direction,
while their shining scales and fluttering fins
glanced in the still water, under the faint gleams
of the wintry sunshine. Hundreds of persons
came to the pier, and dipping in straw-baskets,
lifted them full, and sped to their homes with
the welcome supply. This continued for more
than a week, and the proprietor of the pier,
whose dwelling stood within two hundred yards,
patiently submitted to the annoyance of the eager,
and sometimes quarrelsome crowd, that all might
share in the gift of Providence.

A slight crisp frost, and cold dull weather, had
favoured all these circumstances; but at length a
day of clear and brilliant sunshine, and a sea un-
ruffled by a breath of wind, gave token to those
versed in Shetland meteorology, that the weather
was about to change, and that ere night, a thaw
with a storm of south wind, would scatter the fish,
to be seen there no more. The shoal appeared
yet to be in no degree diminished, and a plan was
concocted by the laird to capture the whole " at
one fell swoop." Nets were not to be had, but
blankets were substituted; many pairs were sewed
together, and by the assistance of stones below, and
ropes above, this novel net was dropped outside

the shoal of sillacks! A score of men in two or three small boats then drew the blanket-net to land. What a sight was then witnessed from the pier!

The ground was covered with sillacks. Every person was permitted to carry off as many as he chose. *Here* was an old man tottering under the weight of his *keyshie** of sillacks, supporting himself on a staff, and often stopping to rest his load on a dyke on the way home. *There* was a youthful widow, her head shrouded in the ample black 'kerchief; shyly she stands aside from the little crowd, till the laird's farm-servant taking her keyshie, fills it (it holds about a bushel), and lifts it on her shoulders, when, with a gentle look of gratitude, but without speaking a word to any one, she hurries back with the acceptable store to her four fatherless boys. Special messengers were dispatched, under the direction of the laird himself, with keyshies full to all the poor within reach, and, finally, all having been served, a number of persons were employed in cleaning and salting the remainder.

During the rest of a very severe winter and spring, the oil from the livers, which is particularly pure and fine, illuminated many a cottage, and the food supplied the wants of many a poor family.

* " *Keyshie*," a straw basket of home manufacture, borne on a person's back by a straw band, passed over the shoulders, in which are carried peats—manure—anything and everything.

And thus, we see, how a kind Providence supplements the scanty products of a sterile soil by abundant supplies from the teeming ocean; and, we think, the poor Shetlanders, in general, are sensible of the blessing, and grateful to the all-bountiful " Giver of every good and perfect gift."

CHAPTER V.

THE PONY.

MANY persons who know nothing whatever of Shetland, know full well a Shetland pony. He is like no other kind of horse, except, perhaps, those in the remotest parts of Norway, and the Cossack steed, to which latter he is so similar, as to induce the belief, that the Shetland race came originally from the Caucasian Mountains, when ODIN and his followers emigrated to Scandinavia. Shetland ponies are chiefly remarkable for their diminutive size, spirit, and hardihood, whereby they set at defiance, want of lodging, wet and hunger, and all other ills incident to a half savage life, in a chill climate, and on an unfertile soil.

Similar remarks will apply also to the cow, the sheep, and the pig. The first is extremely like the Alderney cow, only when giving milk is a little better attended to; the other two, and the pony, all equally wild and savage-looking, are left in a great measure to their own discretion and resources, by the immemorial usage of the country. Every householder, high and low, has from two or three, to twelve or twenty brood mares. They bring forth only every second year, in general, because the foals are not removed from them to be weaned, and thus the mothers are frequently accompanied by their progeny in the husbandry work of the little farms. Provided with pack-saddles, and straw-baskets, they carry out manure, bring the hay, corn, or potatoes, to the barn-yard; but chiefly are they useful during a few weeks at midsummer, for bringing the dried turf or *peats* from the inland moors and hills, to the cottars' dwellings by the sea-side. In this way peats are often carried several miles.

These useful animals are frequently put to severe shifts in foraging for themselves. When their scanty pasture on the common is more than usually bare, they betake themselves to the sea-beach, and feast on tangle and sea-ware; while not a few fall victims in the endeavour to reach some tempting tufts of grass they perceive in the crevices of the banks and precipices. They are rarely ever fed by their owners, except during a long continued snow, and poor fellows, they generally take care to be at hand when weather of this sort is to be expected. Indeed their instincts are so much more prompt and unerring than man's sagacity, or " weather wisdom," that we unhesitatingly calculate on this very circumstance, that the *horses*, old and young, come to their owners' home-stead, or are found standing outside the wicket that leads to the common, immediately before a fall of snow. They are at once admitted, and fed with hay,—if there is any provided,—if not, with dried moor-grass or oat-straw. At the gentlemen's houses there may thus be seen as many as forty; indeed, then, and only then, may the owner see all his stock together at a time. If a foal be weakly, or a colt changing its teeth, it will probably be brought into the kitchen, where the children feed it with oat-cake and sweet-milk, and thus it becomes tame and familiar; so much so, that we have frequently seen the little creatures, if permitted, trot in and out of the parlour rather noisily, to be sure, but with perfect decorum. Some of them are very small, from thirty-three to thirty-six inches high; only once have we seen one so diminutive as thirty inches when full grown, and then it could be carried in a person's arms, and became a welcome, though singular guest, in an English drawing-room! The medium height of the Shetland pony is from thirty-seven to forty inches, and these, when tolerably stout, are in great demand for the North of England coal-mines. No other animal is found so strong for its size, and so easily kept. The consequence is, that in many of the low mining galleries, where human labour was wont to be employed, these active docile creatures are found to answer the purpose much better, so that their price in Shetland has been more than doubled within the last five years. It is to be regretted that Shetlanders generally, are not careful enough to preserve the breed of their ponies pure. The animals, *ad libitum*, are allowed to range wild on the commons, in by far too great numbers for the pastures they have to trust to. Besides, while the strongest and best looking are sold, or taken for

home work, the weak and stunted are left at large
with the mares; consequently the progeny is much
more puny than it otherwise might be. It is true,
a severe winter often becomes a rough regenerator,
by proving fatal to the more feeble animals; and
thus, in this case, as in many others of a different
sort, Nature proves a kind and skilful regenerator
of the breed.

The pony, on the whole, is a droll looking shaggy
creature. When an ostler or groom in England,
gets in charge one of them, fresh from his native
hills and moors, wild and terrified at the unwonted
sounds and sights that greet him, the man believes
him to be something very near of kin to a *brown
bear*, and so eschews all intimate converse with
him; but he soon begins to find the savage is
naturally quiet, gentle, and companionable.

In his native place the pony is very susceptible
of complete domestication. If early brought up
in contact with the cottar's family, as he very often
is, he gets quite as familiar, but never so affectionate and confiding as the dog; for though good
tempered and docile, he is decidedly deficient in
sagacity. We find him running back to his pasture or homestead, when at freedom, even miles
off;—most other domestic animals do the same. If
you should lose your way in a mist, or snow storm,
among the hills and moorland wastes, no very uncommon or pleasant circumstance, just slacken
your bridle rein, and your pony will carry you home
by the best and shortest way. But, on the other
hand, he will very rarely display any definite at-

tachment to those who have been kindest to him, or even appear to know one person from another; and he is selfish, and often lazy. Very frequently he is a bit of a humourist in his way, and indulges in freaks of fun—it may be not altogether to his rider's or owner's satisfaction. Here one will not allow himself to be caught—except by a child— kicking up his heels, and neighing triumphantly at the discomfiture of every older person, however much he may be coaxed. There another makes a point of having the *lead* in every equestrian troop of which he may be one; while his brother, per- haps, is as resolved always toform the *rear-guard.* *This* fellow will not be ridden by a lady, and *that* has equal prejudices against a gentleman. *One* we know, is so exceedingly frolicsome (for he is any- thing but ill-tempered) that he never fails to give every person who attempts to mount him, *one* inti- mate acquaintance with mother earth, if not more, before he sets off decorously on his journey; ex- cepting only from this mark of disrespect, his owner, a young lady, to whom he is invariably most ob- sequious and obedient. Of course, we understand very well, that these humours are the results of the absence of all breaking in or training; neverthe- less we mention them as traits in the natural his- tory of our pony, and, as they hardly ever amount to viciousness, they are to us rather matters of amusement, than anything else. From our ample experience of the dispositions and habits of the Shetland pony, indeed, in this, his unsophisti- cated state, we are persuaded, that any mischievous or vicious propensities, of which we have sometimes heard him accused, have been superinduced by artificial culture and improper management. When he is treated with uniform patience and kindly perseverance, he displays as much tractability and suavity, as other well known and valuable qualities. A good riding pony is *the* great luxury of Shetland life, among the gentry; and it is one they all have in greater or less perfection. Boys and girls easily learn to manage their own steeds. The distances from church, and between the different country mansions, are so great, that walking, especially in winter, is out of the question. Indeed, the Shetlanders seem to consider it not at all necessary or incumbent on them to exercise their own powers of locomotion, when their ponies can carry them any where, so much more swiftly and comfortably. The horses* properly appertaining to each, are great pets with the younger members of a family. All sorts of pretty or uncommon names are chosen for them. Some develop great predeliction for sweetmeats, and others for a piece of bread, for which they will uncouthly seek the hand that caresses them. One of those animals, previously referred to, when on a journey, will, every quarter of an hour or so, turn his head round to his rider, seeking the bit of biscuit which is always provided for him.

They are all exceedingly sure-footed. On diffi-

---

* They are called "*ponies*" in other parts of the world,—not in Shetland.

cult, or very narrow hill-paths, where a stumble
would be most awkward, if not fatal, they carry
their riders with unflagging spirit and steadiness.

Equestrian excursions are the favourite, and indeed only out-of-door recreation, within the Shetlanders reach, at least for ladies, who, in general,
eschew boating.

An equestrian expedition to some favourite
romantic spot—not forgetting the accompaniment
of a couple of well-laden sumpter-ponies, is a most
delightful method of enjoying a long mild summer
day. The ponies seem quite to enter into the
spirit of their riders in a race, or miniature steeple-
chase over the broken ground. Should stranger
visitors be of the party, if tyros, they had better
make up their minds to the mishap of a fall or two;
but this, on the soft grass, or heathy moor, and
from the low stature of the steed, is by no means
a dangerous affair, and soon remedied, when all
are as merry as before.

In fine, the Shetlander could not manage without the pony; and we are proud to think, that our
shaggy and uncouth little countrymen, are deside-
rated also by the fair, the noble, and even the
Royal, in gayer and brighter climes.

CHAPTER VI.

THE ORNITHOLOGIST.

THE following imperfect notices of some of the principal birds to be found in Shetland, aspire not to communicate any thing very strange or novel, far less to be a complete account of our Ornithology, but they may serve to shew the dwellers in more favoured countries, that even amidst scenes the most dreary and remote, pleasant and improving subjects of observation are to be found. In the seclusion of these islands, the families of the gentry, very generally devote much time, and many cares, not only to domestic poultry among other pet animals, but to rearing and taming every sort of wild fowl they may be able to procure young enough from the nest, from the eagle down to the lady-wren, all of which have been subjected to the close observation of the educated Shetlanders.

Of *land birds* there are comparatively few, and the species are those which do not require the shelter of trees, or even of long heather. Hence the sky-lark is the only songster; and for the sportsman who considers none but the *protected birds* worthy of his pursuit, there are no attractions in Shetland. On the other hand, the absence of all restrictions to the most erratic rambles of the visitor, is a discovery rarely made by him, if a *naturalist*, without calling forth his most unqualified approbation. He is never met by surly park-keepers, or circumscribed by oppressive game regulations, or turned aside by lofty walls and thorny hedges, in his pursuit of the objects that interest him. To a few of the more conspicuous of the Shetland birds, the reader's attention is now solicited.

THE EAGLE.

THERE are ten or twelve pairs of the *White-tailed* or *Sea Eagle*, that have nests in these islands. These are chiefly on the west side, where the cliffs are most lofty and inaccessible. Among the undulating hills, however, of the interior of the larger isles, there are many lonely spots, wearing a look of as remote desolation, as if they had been many days' journey from all contact with the doings or the foot-marks of men. There, nature reigns unreclaimed in bare sterile solitude. A coarse brown herbage scantily clothes the peeping gray rocks, like tattered garments on a poverty stricken beggar. A sombre fog creeps over the higher eminences, and a small loch,—though it deserves no more imposing name than that of a pond,—reposes in the hollow of a narrow valley. In such a scene, on a small holm, in the middle of such a stagnant loch, an eagle is sometimes seen on a dull winter day, sitting in solemn contemplation. Perhaps he is resting, while engaged in an extensive excursion, for the locality is far from the nearest eyrie. Truly the *kingly* bird is not likely to be molested by the *autocrat* man, on the lowly, lonely seat he has chosen; and he possibly anticipates the chance, as a tolerable one, that he may pick up a rabbit on the adjacent common. Quite as likely he recollects having frequently, before now, clutched a delicate morsel on this very spot; for here a pair of *red-throated divers* have incubated for a series of years, though the green holm covered with rushes, is not a dozen yards in circumference. At all events there lingers the majestic eagle, unfearing, unscathed, as at home. But see! a wandering pedestrian approaches the spot. He is searching for a stray pony that has proved discontented with his usual pasture or companions. His feet and legs are bare, his head covered with a red woollen cap, which he reverently takes off as he advances, uttering aloud many a holy prayer and approved invocation; and though within a few yards of the *Erne*, casting no more than one scared glance as he hurries on. Reader! there is a fairy knowe, and a haunted well, on the banks of that loch, of which many wild legends are told, and so the Shetlandman has no time, nor does he care to make observations in ornithology, even on the king of birds, whose piercing eye glances surlily at him as he passes.

The gigantic fish called halibut, which is a large species of turbot, often basks, as do other flat fish, near the surface of the sea. The eagle sometimes then pounces upon him, burying his powerful talons in the fish's back. The latter, naturally surprized at an attack so audacious, flounders of course, endeavouring to dive, and thus drown his adversary, or escape his clutches. It is not the habit of our eagle, however, to quit a hold he has once taken; the bravery or pertinacity, if you will, of the *royal spoiler*, forbids so tame a relinquishment of his purpose; so he spreads his mighty wings to balance himself, or to present a greater resistance to the halibut's struggles, or perchance in expectation of being able to carry him off, as was doubtless his primary intention. If the wind or tide be towards land, the eagle's wings act as sails, and he floats on his *floundery* raft, till it grounds with its passenger; when a mightier than either sometimes interferes, and makes them both *his* prey. This was done by an elderly gentleman of the last generation, in the island of Yell, who, as he was taking his evening walk, saw the occurrence as we have described it. Hastening to the water's edge, with his stout walking-stick, he dispatched both eagle and halibut, as exhausted, but still struggling, they were wafted to the shore. Much more recently, a pair of similar incongruous companions, thus murderously associated, were found dead on a beach in Fetlar.

THE SNOWY OWL.

On a stony hill in the middle of the island of Unst, is frequently seen the snowy owl; a noble bird, one of the largest of the *Genus Strix*. It is a native of North America, Lapland, and Norway, but is very rarely observed in Britain, except in the locality we have mentioned, where it is found at all seasons. This hill is plentifully strewed with its pellets,—those balls of feathers and hair, which birds of prey eject from their stomachs, as the indigestible remains of their meals; but after much diligent search, no nests of the snowy owl have been met with, so that it yet remains doubtful whether it breeds in Shetland.

The peasants here have a superstitious dislike to these birds, and avoid, rather than seek to molest them; though on several occasions they have been caught and kept for some time in a domestic state. The adult male snowy owl is a beautiful bird, nearly quite white; the female is much the larger, and pretty thickly spotted with dusky gray. The eyes are large, of a bright yellow colour, and very intelligent; the gait in walking is exceedingly awkward, but the pinions are of remarkable size and strength.

A very fine pair of snowy owls, captured in Unst, are now in the Zoological Gardens, London. They were easily tamed, and not at all nice in their tastes,—though mice, rabbits, and small birds, newly killed, were evidently preferred.

THE RAVEN.

OF rapacious birds, the *Genus Corvus* is in Shetland, beyond comparison, the most destructive; but of these, there are only resident, the *Corbie* (raven) and the *Hoodie Crow*. The former builds in the lofty cliffs, the only bird so aspiring as to rival the eagle in the sublimity of his dwelling-place.

It was long supposed that the raven preyed on

carrion only, or if he attacked any of the quadrupeds, it was when they were quite exhausted, or
dying. But of late he has been found frequently
to destroy even ponies in comparative strength;
though it must be confessed, such instances occur
only in spring, when the animals on the commons
are weakened by the hardships of winter, and the
birds are feeding their young. *Corbie* sees a
pony lying down to rest, or standing listless and
forlorn-looking near a dyke; with an impatient
croak he darts down, and at one stroke pierces the
eye of the poor animal, which immediately rolls
itself in its agony, generally with the injured eye
next to the ground. This leaves the other eye a
mark for the murderer, and another stroke blinds
his victim. A third attack is made about the tail,
and then he soars away, with his malign, triumphant,
croak, croak, croak. He knows that he has given
the poor pony his death wound, and he will return in a few days to the carrion, which it is decidedly the best policy to leave for his use, that he
may be driven the less to create new prey in a
similar manner.

Newly dropt lambs, goslings, and other domestic
poultry, are, however, still more extensively victims of the voracious crows and ravens. The
" Commissioners of Supply," in former years, rewarded with a premium, *per head,* any person who
destroyed these audacious birds; and it were
greatly to be desired, that this philanthropic practice were recurred to; for, in certain districts, the
mischief and loss are incalculable.

THE STARLING,

LARGE flocks of starlings are constantly seen in Shetland. They are the most familiar birds we have, standing us in stead of the robin, and other songsters, whose notes they often adopt with great glee and precision. Pert they are, hopping about every where, to share in the *dole* of all the household pets, from the favourite colt's sly sheaf of corn, to the milk-curd provided for the tame seagull. The starling, however, is never mischievous, and is not only patiently tolerated, but even regarded with good will, as he feeds on destructive insects, and *debris* of all kinds. When domesticated, he is a particularly amusing fellow, and very affectionate to his protectors.

THE MOUNTAIN LINNET.

THIS is another, though much smaller bird, that frequents our fields in extensive flocks, but to which no such favour or mercy is shown. It is called by ornithologists *Tringilla Montana ;* in the vernacular, it is *Linty.* This bird is particularly fond of turnip-seed ; and when the turnip-plant begins to spring (the seed being on the top of the peeping leaf) swarms of *linties* congregate on the furrows, and in a short time whole rows of the embryo turnips are pulled up, and scattered on the ground like heaps of ravelled white threads. Great numbers of these birds are shot down while thus depredating on a turnip-field, and in their crops are sometimes found above two hundred of the seminal leaves. The mischief hence arising to the miniature fields of the cottars may be imagined. Indeed, a return need not be expected, unless the ground be diligently watched till the plants are all fairly above the soil.

THE GOLDEN CRESTED WREN.

WHO would imagine that this smallest and most beautiful of British birds, could weather the damp atmosphere, and heavy blasts of Shetland! Yet it is frequently found here at all seasons. Sometimes indeed it is picked up lifeless on the common, dashed perhaps by a storm against the stony ground. At other times it flies into the house by some open door or window for shelter, most likely from a hawk. When we mark the delicate frame and bright plumage of the tiny wren, our thoughts dwell not on our own bare hills and turf-dykes, and inhospitable climate, but wander away to those bright bowers and flowery gardens which are the appropriate dwelling-place of our solitary visitor; but we ever welcome the brave and sweet little wren, associated as it is with soft scenery and brilliant skies—of which many a dweller in these bleak isles may dream, but never see.

THE GOLDEN PLOVER.

GREAT numbers of these birds frequent our loneliest hills and valleys. Sometimes the flocks are so numerous, that the ground is thickly covered with them for a considerable space, and the air darkened as they rise on wing. They are exceedingly wild, however, which may be accounted for by the fact, that every one who can use a fowling-piece, pursues them as an acceptable dainty for the table. The plovers are always observed to allow one or more *equestrians* to pass them within twenty yards; but should a solitary sportsman with a gun be in the way, they keep at a distance so respect-ful, that he may follow them many a weary mile without ever getting a shot at them.

THE ROCK PIGEON.

IN those parts of the islands, the rudest and most inaccessible, where the full force of the sea meets the rocky shore, the latter is, as we have pre-viously noticed, broken into a thousand fantastic forms, deep recesses and tortuous caverns. Into these latter, as the tide rushes and rages, no man who has any regard for his life will ever venture with his boat. But in the eaves of the wave-worn apertures, the rock pigeons, in innumerable flocks, build and roost. This rare bird is considered to be the original stock of the numerous varieties of the tame dove. In small flocks it visits the fields in spring and autumn, feeding chiefly on roots and larvae turned up by the spade, or amongst the stubble. Not unfrequently a young bird in its thoughtlessness or inexperience, has been enticed to remain at the dove-cot of some *cultivated* and *civilized* congeners, with which it has formed ac-quaintance. Here it has mated, and become a parent, retaining much of its native shyness and timidity, but infusing into the domestic broods a welcome variety of plumage, as well as a decided gracefulness of mein and hardihood of constitution. The tame pigeon thrives very well in Shetland, but has not so many broods in the season, as in more favoured latitudes.

THE CORN-CRAKE.

WE have remarked, that there are neither grouse nor partridges in Shetland. The only bird of their genus is the *Land-rail* or *Corn-crake*. It is as the cuckoo to the Shetlanders. Its monotonous call is most grateful to them, and they will not suffer it to be molested or destroyed, because they believe its presence foretells a good crop. This is not, however, mere superstition; for, as they are delicate birds, when they breed and thrive it shows the season to be mild, and probably, therefore, the corn will grow and ripen well. In Shetland the corn-crake usually builds, not among the corn, as in other places, that being too low and backward, but in the more early rye-grass and meadow-fields, where, in hay-harvest, its nest, if found, is heedfully respected.

Connecting the *Land Birds* with the *Swimmers*, or those living for the most part in the water, are the *Waders*. Of these there are numerous varieties in Shetland, most interesting in their habits, and every where accessible to observation. Long legs bare of feathers, long necks and bills also, and small elegantly shaped bodies, are the distinguishing characteristics of all this class, from the diminutive *Sandpiper* to the stately *Heron*.

Walking on an evening along the flat beach, near the confluence of a narrow brook with the sea, or perchance wandering on the shore of one of the solitary lakelets we have before described, you may often see a *Heron*. He has waded a yard or so into the water, and looks into it intently; then he plunges in his head, and you can soon perceive him swallowing a good-sized trout. Again he watches patiently, then another dip, and he raises a freshwater eel. You have now a fancy to interrupt his agreeable occupation, and run towards him with a shout;—you do not intend to harm him, poor fellow! but just want to see how he can fly. With an effort that looks like laziness or repletion, the eel still struggling between his mandibles, the *Haigrie* (for so he is called in Shetland) stretches his enormous wings, and you can see how disproportionately small the body is to the extensive pinions, neck, and legs. Slowly he rises, *flap, flap, flapping* his wings, like the sails of a windmill, till he reaches a quieter spot at a short distance, where he alights, and finishes his meal.

Except to observe that a sportsman will find some good *snipe-shooting* in various districts, we shall not say more of the *wading* birds, but hasten to notice a few of the numerous class of sea-fowl—those

> " Who, like nations, annual come and go,
>   And like the living clouds on clouds arise,
>   Infinite wings! till all the plume-dark air,
>   And rude resounding shores, are one wild cry."

Here every step of the Naturalist is "marked with pleasantness;" but we intend to notice only some traits, which are more evident to the resident or native observer, than to any mere wandering tourist, however intelligent and zealous.

THE SWAN.

Of this magnificent bird we have passing visits only. The wild species does not inhabit any part of the British Islands, but chooses the most inaccessible solitudes of the " Far North" for the purpose of bringing forth and rearing its young, and then migrates to the latitude of Southern Europe to spend the winter. A few of these beautiful creatures often rest on our sequestered lochs and pools, on their way to and from the Arctic Regions; in spring going thither, in autumn returning South. They fly as wild geese do, in the form of a wedge, the apex being occupied by a leader; and as they fly, they utter a clear sonorous cry, which is often heard when we cannot see the æronaut voyagers. In a still evening or morning, it has a singular and even harmonious effect, breathing, as it does, the very essence of expectation and encouragement to each other; and to the Shetlander, in the early season, it is the cheering voice of returning spring. It rarely happens when a few swans alight to rest on one of our small lakes or voes, that they escape without leaving a few victims sacrificed to man's cupidity. The purity, lightness, and warmth of their breast of down, make the skin a saleable and valuable commodity, while the flesh is a substantial dainty, tasting like excellent mutton.

THE GOOSE.

CONCERNING geese our observations relate only to the tame or domestic variety, which may be ranked as " sea-fowl," inasmuch, as in many places, flocks of them may be constantly seen enjoying themselves in the sea, near the head of some sheltered voe ; and these are observed to be particularly thriving.

Great numbers of geese are reared by the Shetland cottars, because as *they* manage the matter, the birds give no trouble, and are a source of considerable profit. They feed on the uninclosed lands or commons, receiving hardly any attention from their owners, from the moment the broods newly hatched are set at liberty, till brought home at Martinmas to be slaughtered and cured for winter provision.

A curious sight may be witnessed in the Shetland cottages during the months of March and April. You enter the outer or " *butt* end," as it is called ; the peat fire burns on a raised hearth in the midst of the earthen floor, the blackened rafters are scarcely visible for the clouds of smoke, which escape as they best may, by several holes in the thatched roof. When your eyes have become a little accustomed to the obscure atmosphere,—which, be it observed in extenuation, is far from being so choking and unpleasant as if coal, or even wood, were the fuel,—you will perceive, ranged along one wall, a row of dark-looking cells, built of turf, the inhabitants, or the use of which, it would probably puzzle many a natural philosopher to divine. Perhaps you are accompanied by a canine attendant, which less ceremoniously polite than yourself, after having exchanged a growl or two with sundry curs of his own species, begins to explore the mysterious cells, which to his wisdom, look very suspicious. When he has poked his nose into a very small aperture, a mighty sigh is heard, which, as he persists, is succeeded by an unearthly scream, echoed by half a dozen additional voices in chorus. These are the alarmed cries of the maternal *geese*, each occupying her own hut, and carefully watched over by the family of the fisherman, more as a matter of excellent amusement, than a point of duty, or even of interest. When the goslings are hatched, the broods, with their mothers, are fed for a few days, and then are brought out to the gander, and year-old birds which do not incubate. A joyful recognition and greeting take place, and with loud and long continued congratulations, the paternal guide leads his large family to the common. By the way, we may just stop a moment to remark, that the proverb respecting the " *stupidity of the goose,*" is neither more nor less than a *gross libel.* No animals can be more sagacious and gentle to their protectors, and more social and affectionate one with another. Generally as many as sixty goslings may be sent forth from the cottar's dwelling, as we have described, of which not above a half ever return ; but as there are no markets within reach, and the animals are therefore useful merely for home consumption, their owners do not consider the flocks worth the expense and trouble of more minute attention. The feathers are almost always sold to the small traders, for it is very rarely the cottagers sleep on any thing but straw, their scanty resources compelling them to turn whatever they can into absolute necessaries.

THE GREAT NORTHERN DIVER.

THIS majestic and beautiful bird is quite as large as a tame goose. Its breast is of snowy white, the back a dusky brown, mottled with spots of white, and it has beautiful bars of black around its neck. Its breeding-places are Greenland, Iceland, and Lapland, and it is found in Shetland only during the winter, when in stormy weather two or three may often be seen close to the shore, in some sheltered bay or creek. It is rarely observed to fly, but when disturbed, dives, and is seen no more. In company with these handsome birds, there are generally some of the same size, but different in plumage, being all over, except the breast, of a brown colour. These were long called *Immer Geese;* but a Shetland Ornithologist profiting by the favourable opportunities for observing them, discovered that the so-called *geese* were merely the young of the Northern Diver.

It appears singular, indeed, to those unacquainted with sea-fowl in their native retreats, and it has frequently puzzled Naturalists in their attempts at classification, that the plumage of several species *changes* according to age. Most of the gull tribes, for example, are indiscriminately mottled grey in their first year, and are vernacularly called in Shetland by one name, *Scorie*. They are then good for food, being tender, and by no means *fishy* in taste. For the next two or three years the feathers gradually become of a lighter colour, but still those of a size cannot be distinguished as to species. In the fourth year the breast is clad in its spotless white; the greyish blue appears on the backs of the *Iceland* and *Herring Gulls*, and the deep brown on those of the two species known as the " Greater" and " Lesser Black-backed Gulls." The Skua Gull alone is altogether and always brown.

THE SKUA GULL.

THIS is another rare bird, a native of the Shetland Isles, and much asked after by Ornithologists. It is one of the largest of the gull tribe, and as we observed above, of a dark brown colour. From the unsparing depredations of collectors, this family of birds was nearly extinct, being, in the locality where they were most numerous, reduced to three individuals; but by the persevering protection of the proprietor of the soil, they have now increased to above thirty pairs. The promontory, or inclosure here alluded to, is Hermaness, the most northerly point of the British Islands; and during summer no sight can possibly be more interesting and animated than what is here presented. The whole ground,— as well as the precipitous banks, which on three sides overhang the sea,—is literally covered with innumerable nests of the various species of water-fowl, so that the unwonted visitor is apt to tread on them before he is aware, and is each moment in danger of being struck by the wings of the parent birds, which alarmed for the safety of their progeny, dash over his head, and almost in his face, with screams that are absolutely deafening. Contrasted with this animated picture, when these birds have migrated for the winter, how bleak and desolate is the aspect of the scenery, from whence such multitudes of inhabitants of the rock and sea have fled for a time, leaving only a forlorn wilderness, which erewhile had swarmed with innocent and lovely forms of busy life, engaged in their most interesting and important avocations!

From the nests in Hermaness Skua Gulls have been occasionally procured and domesticated. He is not, however, an amiable bird, and is apt to be tyrannical and fierce to poultry, and even to children. His motions and cry, as well as disposition, are not unlike those of the eagle; and for his size, his strength is almost as remarkable. In the artificial state of domestication, he will feed on almost any thing, and though fish, of course, is his natural aliment, he always prefers flesh, and even carrion, from the hands of men.

THE HERRING GULL,

Or common *Sea-Mew*, is so well known, and universally diffused, that any particulars of its history might seem superfluous. One curious trait only, therefore, shall be related, and that because of its exclusive connection,—so far at least as we are aware,—with scenes of Shetland.

The circumstance to which we refer, is the pertinacity with which the herring gull takes on itself the guardianship of the seals, from their most formidable enemy—man. If a flock of seals is reposing on the rocks, and danger approaches, the herring gulls immediately set up an alarm-cry; warily the hunter creeps onwards, taking care to keep to *leeward* of his quarry. The seals are sleeping securely, one only acting as sentinel. When he hears the call of the gulls, he generally raises his head, and looks anxiously around, snuffing the air; but as he can see, hear, or smell nothing suspicious, he begins again to fan and stroke himself with his flippers, evincing the most tranquil enjoyment. But the gulls continue screaming, and flying lower and lower, circling even round the sportman's head; and at length, in the desperation of their anxiety, they dash into the very midst of the sleeping seals, which latter demonstration of course awakes the objects of their care, which start off into the sea, and instantly disappear.

The cause or object of the herring gull in this often observed procedure, cannot be ascertained. It may not be ascribed to *instinct*, since it can have little direct reference to the bird's own circumstances, and that little, is adverse to its interest. If it is sagacity, it is surely an instance of its exercise quite *unique*, that one order of animal should expose itself to imminent danger, in warning another to escape the same ; and we regret to say, the self-constituted guard often falls a victim to his disinterestedness ; for the sportsman, disappointed of his prey, generally discharges his spleen and his ready weapon, so as fatally to revenge the unwarranted interference of the pragmatical gulls.

THE KITTIWAKE.

SOME of the most precipitous cliffs on the north and west of Shetland are entirely appropriated by this, one of the smallest and most beautiful of the gull *genus*. Imagine a wall of rock several hundred feet high, on the slight shelving projections of which, sit tens of thousands of these gentle and lovely creatures. The adult birds are pure white, with a light greyish blue shade on the back. They are busy with their young; two little black heads peep from every nest, to and from which the parents incessantly flutter with an anxious care,— a tender vigilance most affecting to witness. Fire a gun in the face of the precipice; what a cry and clouding of the air succeed, as the alarmed denizens start off from their perch !—a few yards only, however ; for momentarily and swiftly they return to their nurslings. Fire again, and the clamour is still greater, the flight even shorter, while many resolutely remain at the parental post ; and we have repeatedly seen them shot rather than leave their nests unguarded.

Pass onward in your boat to the base of the next similar cliff ; it too is thickly peopled from top to bottom, but its inhabitants, though of the same size and plumage, are much quieter than those you have already seen. They seem to prefer remaining in contemplative enjoyment of the wild sequestered scenery, the bright sunshine, and the healthful sea-breeze, except when one or two are absent on occasional foraging expeditions.

These are kittiwakes of a year old ; they are not bringing forth this season; they congregate together as brethren, and not until next summer will they return to the cliff where they were hatched, to become parents in their turn. They are called by the fishermen " *Yield Kittiwakes*," and are remorselessly murdered by every one that has time, and can use a fowling-piece; for we can assure the reader, that a broiled kittiwake of this sort, eats almost as delicately as a partridge.

THE CORMORANT.

ON the lower and on the more detached rocks, and on every pinnacle of stone indeed, that peeps above water, sit the *Shags*. Their *congeners*, the *Cormorants*, affect a position considerably more elevated. In Shetland they are all called *Scarfs*. They are of a bluish shining black, are gaunt and ominous looking, and utter most discordant cries. The cormorant is the larger species. When young, its breast is white, but this gradually disappears, leaving on the adult bird only a small white spot on the thigh. The shag is of a dark greyish brown in his first year, but afterwards becomes all black, and is similar to the cormorant in shape, but much smaller. Most sea-fowl eggs are palatable and wholesome food, but those of this genus are quite unfit to eat, and have a most fetid odour.

Unpromising as these birds would appear, they are easily tamed, and none are more docile, sagacious, and affectionate. We have had a cormorant in a domestic state for some time. It went on the sea and fished for itself, but instantly returned if its owner called, following him with a plaintive note, and seeking, with every possible gesture of fondness to be carressed. While gentle and courteous to every one who noticed it, its discriminating attachment to its master was most conspicuous. In his absence it watched his return from the top of a gateway, and distinguished him at a considerable distance. This interesting favourite pined and died after some weeks of suffering. When the body was opened, the lungs were found quite decayed from tubercular disease.

The fishermen take these birds whenever they have opportunity. While fishing for sillacks they often bait a strong hook with one of the newly caught little fish, and make it move invitingly just beneath the surface of the water. The scarf seizes the sillack, and in attempting to swallow it, is caught by the hook, and by means of the long rod, is held down until drowned.

Another and more whimsical method in which scarfs are caught, is the following :—On a dark night, when the densely peopled rocks and cliffs are wrapped in silence and rest, and no doubt the inhabitants, in the security of their wisdom, think *men* are, or ought to be, sleeping too, a small boat approaches the base of the rocks. The men carry a *great iron pot*, filled with peat fire, which they suddenly uncover, maintaining the while strict silence. The scarfs, poor fellows, awake suddenly, and cannot imagine what this may mean. In the confusion of ideas consequent on their disturbance, or in their eagerness to greet the dawning morn, which has thus surprized them, they fly directly at the light, even quite into the boat, and of course into the clutches of their cunning enemies, who are always particularly amused, as well as gratified at the success of their stratagem, and the simplicity with which the poor scarfs rush on their doom.

CHAPTER VII.

FALLEN ANGELS.

WHO except a Shetlander would detect, under this ominous designation, those curious and most interesting creatures, THE SEALS,—the only denizens of many a wild nook in these islands, and whose history and habits, therefore, may be more conveniently studied here, than any where else, at least in Britain. From their shyness, their great strength, and the singular intelligence of their aspect, the Shetland fishermen imagine them to be fallen spirits in metempsychosis, enduring in the form of seals a mitigated punishment. For this reason, however eagerly they may be killed for the sake of their valuable skins and blubber, it is generally done not without compunction and misgivings, it being supposed that they are both powerful to injure, and malevolent to revenge. The following is one wild legend selected from others on this subject, that circulate among the Shetland fishers.

A man gathering shell-fish for bait one morning, having found a full-grown seal, lying on a low rock, managed to get between it and the sea, and attacked it with the small narrow spade with which the people here dig for mussels, and other shell-fish.

A dexterous stroke or two on the head effectually
stunned the poor seal, and the victor immediately
proceeded to skin his prey, greatly desiring to
have a few pairs of moccasins (vernacularly, *rivlins*)
from the tough and beautiful skin.   Having accomplished this, he tossed the carcase into the
sea, and hurried to his companions, who were im-
patiently awaiting him, in order to proceed to
their fishing.

Meanwhile the seal having only been stunned
and stripped, soon revived to feel, as may be supposed, particularly cold, and still more disconsolate
at his changed and disfigured condition.   Sad and
miserable he wandered through the waters lament-
ing, avoided by friends and lovers, and scoffed at
by many erewhile insignificant foes.   In this
plight he retired to the neighbourhood of a coral
bower, where a mermaid had her abode.   The latter overheard the sad plaint of the cruelly used
seal, and after kindly soothing, asked if she could
help him.   *Selkie* imagined she might, but only by
regaining for him the covering of which he had
been so ruthlessly bereft.   Whereupon, like a pitying angel, the kind and gentle being darted off on
her compassionate and friendly errand.

Now the spoiler's conscience had by this time
sorely smitten him for having destroyed the seal
that morning; he believed some evil would as-
suredly overtake him; he muttered many a prayer
and many a vow, and carefully concealed his fault
from his comrades, giving them to understand, that
he had obtained the much coveted skin from an

animal he had found dead on the shore. How hor-
rified then was he, when a hook on their fishing-
lines drew into their boat a mermaid!

Eagerly he implored the other men to release
her instantly; but they over-ruled his wishes, from
the conviction that they would obtain a considerable reward for such an extraordinary capture. The
mermaid was therefore consigned to a secure place
in the boat, and laid carefully on *the skin of the seal*,
that very prize for which she had thus risked her life.
After a few plaintive cries, the self-devoted maiden
of the sea began to feel, that out of her native
element she could not long survive, and that she
would soon indeed fall a victim to her friendship;
but at the sametime, she well knew, the demons of
the deep would avenge her, and that when the
boat had sunk to the caves and groves below,
though all too late for her, the seal would find his
robe again. It so proved accordingly. The mermaid had hardly gasped her last, when a sudden
and terrific storm arose. In the hurry and alarm
of the moment, the men forgot their late prey;
but the murderer of the seal believed firmly his
hour was come, and that the associates of the
" fallen angel" were busy at their demon work of
revenge.

The boat was lost with all her crew.

When she sunk in the whelming billows, the
unhappy seal recovered his clothing, but had to
lament over the dead body of his devoted friend.

For this reason, the seals have ever since consti-
tuted themselves the especial guardians of the mer-

F

maiden race. They watch them with grateful soli-
citude,—often supply them with dainties from
dangerous deeps, where mermaids may not venture ; and while frequently themselves charmed
listeners of the sea-maids' wondrous songs, never
remit a vigilant guard over their safety, or neglect
to give prompt alarm should danger approach.
Indeed, it often happens, that seals fall victims to
this self-imposed task, thus repaying the dearly dis-
played-devotion of a mermaid to one of their race.

A few more authentic memoirs of the seal will
prove interesting enough, we hope, without farther
additions from such " legendary lore."

The seal, we presume, is well known to be an
amphibious, but warm-blooded animal. It breathes
through lungs, and therefore, of course, requires
atmospheric air, as necessarily as the terrestrial creatures, though it may survive for fifteen or twenty
minutes without respiration. It brings forth a
single young one at a birth, which it suckles. Its
thick and tough skin is covered with a close, short,
and often beautifully variegated crop of hair. Immediately under the skin is a thick layer of fat,
like that of the pig, so that it has been called the
Sea Hog, and also the *Sea Dog*. These characteristics would place the seal amongst the *mam-
malia*, where, indeed, it is generally classed ; while,
on the other hand, it is of the shape, and furnished
with paws very much resembling the fins of a fish ;
it inhabits the vast ocean, and its stormy coasts,
and its food consists exclusively of fish, and other
sea produce.

There are but two species of seals that frequent the British coasts, well marked in their size, habitat, and instincts. They are distinguished as the Greater and Lesser Seal, *Phoca Barbata*, and *Phoca Vitulina*. Two other species are found, however, in Greenland and Hudson's Bay; and occasional individuals have been seen in an emaciated state, or washed ashore dead on our coasts. These are called the *Hooded Seal*, and the *Harp Seal;* the former, because of a bladder-like appendage on its forehead, and the latter, from a beautiful dark marking the shape of a harp on its side, the rest of the skin being nearly white.

The Phoca Barbata is never above ten feet in length, more usually it is seven or eight; and yet it has been often stated at twenty. The mistake has probably arisen from confounding the appearance of a *walrus* with a seal. The former has a head hardly larger than that of a seal, and otherwise much resembles it when seen only at sea, but it is more than twice as large in the body, and otherwise a very different animal.

The male of our *Greater Seal* is larger, and much darker in colour than the female; he also grows darker with age, while the female becomes lighter, and the *physiognomy* of each sex is so marked, as to be at once recognised by any person who has opportunities of seeing them in their native haunts. Moreover, the Greater Seals live by pairs in some wild caverns, and inhabit the same spot for many successive seasons. The Lesser Seals, on the contrary, congregate in con-

siderable flocks. They frequent sheltered bays,
and low lying shores, and often ascend the estuaries
and larger rivers of Britain. This species is never
above six feet long ; nor can the male be distinguished from the female at a glance like the others.
Their colour is also more speckled, and the head
shorter and rounder in proportion.

All seals are extremely wild, and of prodigious
muscular strength. They delight to sport among
the breakers, the whirls of the Northern Ocean
and its fiercest hurricanes being their pastime and
diapasons. The eye is large, dark, and instinct
with sagacity, we had almost said—*feeling*, more
proud and fierce in its expression than that of the
gazelle, yet hardly less beautiful.

The writer has lived in a family where a young
female seal of the larger species was domesticated.
The prejudice of the lower classes could not be
overcome ; they looked on the unoffending creature
with astonishment and loathing, which no elo-
quence could conquer. One female servant only
could be prevailed on to attend to the animal, which
permitted her any familiarity, though it kept all
other persons at a respectful distance. The flashing glance of her full brilliant eye was indeed of
itself sufficient to awe the boldest that approached
her, especially when her great strength was considered, which every motion and gesture plainly
revealed. But in fact the creature was invariably
inoffensive and unassuming. Being allowed to go
where she pleased, she occasionally hobbled up and
down stairs, looking into every chamber, as if to

gratify an insatiable curiosity. When she got into
a novel position, she would remain quite still for a
long time, examining every object, in the way an
American Indian might do, when first beholding the
appurtenances of civilized life. On one occasion
she was discovered intently gazing into the cradle
where lay a sleeping infant. But into the human
eye and countenance this seal would steadfastly
stare, as if seeking to hold communion with the
inmost spirit. This at least was the impression
invariably made, and hardly to be withstood,
amounting almost to fascination, till, in truth, even
educated persons have imagined it such a "pleasing
dread" as that with which one might look on
" archangel ruined," and perhaps justifying the
fishermen's appellation with which we headed this
sketch.

She often gave utterance to the most mournful
sounds, wild and sad enough to dispose one to
weep at times, and even startling to a stranger.
They could not have been awakened by memories
of freedom and the storm, for she had been taken
from her nursery cave when only a few days old,
ere she had sniffed the breeze, or tasted the brine.
It must then have been *seals' music;* it was similar
to what the hunter listens for when on a still summer day he intrudes on their homes among the
rocks and caves.

This household seal ate great quantities of fish—
a hundred and twenty sillacks, for example, hardly
afforded her a sufficient supper. But she was soon
permitted to cater for herself, and every day when

the door of her apartment was opened for her,
repaired to the sea, where, after enjoying herself
for a while, she would answer with her mournful
prolonged cry, the voice of kindness calling her to
return. Then she would hasten to land, and follow
her friend, expressing fondness in her own pensive
and somewhat uncouth way, for the draught of
new milk she seemed to prefer to every thing else.
This interesting protegé, when full grown, and
quite domesticated, fell a victim to an accident, to
the great regret of the family, while the cottage
neighbours rejoiced in the absence of what they
believed a being beyond humanity—" *an unchancey
brute.*"

A few months thereafter another young seal was
captured in a singular and interesting manner.
Let the reader imagine a long narrow arm of the
North Sea; on each side the rocks are rugged and
precipitous, and of considerable height. Deep in-
dentations all along the shore form low-browed
caverns, where several pairs of the Great Seal
live and bring up their young almost unmolested.
The openings into some of these caves are so low,
that they can only be entered at neap tides;
into others a boat may row, or be warped, if the
sea is quite smooth; while others again are only
accessible by the seals themselves, deep under the
clear green water. Into all of them the sea flows
with a hollow gurgling swell, on which a boat rises
and falls somewhat fearfully, even when the water
outside is quite still. At the inner extremity is a
pebbly beach, generally in total darkness, so deep

and tortuous is the approach. Sometimes the cave is more open and spacious, but so much the more terrific, in that case, is the long roll of the billow, which bursting on the circumscribed beach, echoes in thundering reverberations from the overhanging cliffs.

Such are the seals' homes. But sometimes, either because better places are pre-occupied, or from caprice, or some other cause, they choose less feasible dwelling-places, as the following anecdote will show :—

A fisherman was one day engaged in gathering limpets for bait, having descended from above into a narrow creek on the wildest side of the arm of the sea we have described. The water in the geo was deep, but the latter terminated, like the caves, in a stony beach. On either side the rock of gneiss rose in dark masses, and lay in loose fragments at the base, except at one point where the man had scrambled down to reach the water's edge. To his great surprize he saw a young seal lying on the smoothest part of the little beach at the end of the geo. It ought, perhaps, to be mentioned here, that the young of the *Barbata* does not take the water for several weeks after birth, while that of the *Vitulina* plunges into the sea with the mother immediately.

The parents of the young seal were swimming in the geo; the male (one of the very largest) was sporting in unsuspecting security in the surge; the female more vigilant, was soon half on shore, as she descried the intruder. Then looking savagely at

him, with her large fierce eyes, she plunged again
into the deep water, and seemed to bespeak the
assistance of her mate, when both came nearer to see
the spoiler of their home, who, in the meantime,
had caught the young one by the hinder flipper
(half paw and half fin), and in spite of its struggles,
managed to bind it fast to a stone with a piece of
rope he fortunately happened to have with him.
He then ran to the nearest cottage, and dispatched
a messenger to his landlord for instructions. Returning to the geo, he remained more than two
hours watching his captive, and observing with interest, not unmixed with compunction, its futile
attempts to escape, and the anxious affectionate
gestures of the parents. Very few of his class in
Shetland would have ventured into a similar situation, far less remained so long in it, amid the wild
solitude, the booming surf, the plaintive wail of the
young one, the frantic plunging and loud howl of
the parents, and the fast approach of evening.
Still our fisherman kept his singular guard, and
just as darkness was closing in upon him, messengers arrived, with orders not to hurt the old seals,
but by all means to secure the young one. This
required the strength of three stout men, but it was
at last safely accomplished, and the captive speedily
transferred to a country gentleman's residence.
It obstinately refused food and drink for several
days; then it took some new milk, and at length
began to eat fish, and was allowed to go to the
sea for a daily bathe, not, however, without being
secured by a rope attached to his flipper. On one

occasion the line slipped off;—freedom—the track-
less ocean, and communion with his own kind were
all before him. He tumbled about and dived, and
it was thought was gone for ever; but the person
who attended to him continuing to call him in the
caressing tone he was accustomed to, the noble
animal at length rushed on shore to the servant's
feet, and followed to his sleeping place like the
most affectionate dog. To all other persons, however, this seal was not merely sullen, but fierce.
During a three days absence of the usual attendant, neither kindness nor force could induce him
to swallow the least nourishment, and his joy at
his friend's return was demonstrated in the most
unequivocal manner, proving beyond a doubt that
the most savage natures are sensible of, and grateful for, continued gentleness and kind offices.
To conclude the short history of our Phoca, he
lived in captivity eight or ten months, and it was
hoped was becoming gradually more gentle and
confiding, when all at once he refused food, and
even liberty when offered to him. For *twenty-
eight days* he took neither meat nor drink! Till
within the last six days, his strength seemed quite
unabated, though his plumpness rapidly diminished.
At length he died, and it appeared he had swallowed something that impeded digestion.

Does any reader not altogether approve of sub-
jecting such animals to a state of domestication so
unnatural? May not something be said by way
of reply, in favour of that spirit of enquiry into
their habits and dispositions, which such experi-

ments tend to satisfy. And yet, after so many attempts to tame the seal, as we know have been made, and with the gentlest kindest skill, we are bound to confess, we very much prefer to see these noble and beautiful animals enjoying their wild sports and freedom among their native rocks and caves.

CHAPTER VIII.

AN EXCURSION.

A FEW years ago, early in the month of August, a large family circle in the most northerly of the Shetland Isles, were rejoicing in the society of one of their number, from whom they had been separated for upwards of forty years. He left his native country at the age of fifteen; he revisited it for the first time, when grey-headed, and a grandfather, and yet he still retained all the freshness and purity of early associations; an observation very generally made of the long absent Shetlander. It was to cherish, and more deeply imprint these sentiments, that all of the family that now remained on earth, were gathered under one roof for the short period of his sojourn.

One fine evening, soon after the glad reunion, it was proposed, that the whole party (of which the writer was one), should next day have a boating excursion round the northern promontory of the island, which is also the most northerly point of the British Empire. Here the creeks and caves, and lofty cliffs, tenanted by myriads of sea-fowl, were objects which, besides their great natural attractions of wild and grand sublimity, were en-

deared to the elder members of the group, by many
early and happy recollections ; and there were, besides, new connections, and young branches, that
were desirous to visit them.

The following morning was most propitious to
our wishes, and all agreed, that a Shetland sky is
sometimes as clear, and a Shetland sun as bright,
as they generally are in more favoured latitudes.

After an early breakfast, the ponies were got
ready for a ride of four miles to the place of em-
barkation.

The steeds were all fine specimens of our docile
and spirited little countrymen.

One of the ladies was mounted on a young and
beautiful black one, which had never before been
subjected to saddle or bridle, having been brought
but a few days previously, wild from his native
hills.

Our way lay over a hill of rocky serpentine, and
the first object of attraction to the long banished
one, was a quarry of chromate of iron, which had
been discovered during his absence. The excava-
tion here was of considerable depth, the chrome
ore lying embedded in veins, through the serpentine, apparently in great abundance, and in the
working of it giving employment during the summer season to many men and lads. On descend-
ing to a level valley, on the other side of the hill,
the numerous party dispersed a little ; the elder
members taking the smoother and straighter course,
while the younger sought difficulties in a rougher
and more eccentric path for the pleasure of sur-

mounting them. All were, however, within sight
of each other, when the young pony we mentioned, treated his rider to a full gallop over the plain.
All-unaccustomed to the intent of bit or rein, no
restraint or coaxing could stop his frolicsome career,
and the rest of his rider's companions put their steeds
likewise to the gallop, supposing she meant to chal-
lenge them to a race. Away went the whole troop
in a most alarming pell-mell style; and it was well,
they were all experienced and fearless equestrians,
as indeed most of the Shetland gentry are, even from
childhood. The head-strong colt accomplished his
race in gallant style, keeping ahead of all compe-
titors, and never slackening his space till he reached
and passed the advanced group of horsemen,
startling them from their sober propriety of pace,
by his headlong approach, when he halted of his
own accord, with a loud neigh, as if in triumph
that he had overtaken the foremost. All the
ponies and cattle in Shetland have their own appropriate names; for example, we had among us,
a *Murphy*, because, when a foal, he was fed during
a severe winter entirely on potatoes; a *Herman*,
from the pasture-land he most frequented; a *Hus-
cussay*, from the island of his birth-place; and two
of the youngsters, who had been studying Scandinavian antiquities, chose to give their pet-steeds
the classical names of *Sigmund* and *Thora*. Our
racer, therefore, which had not yet acquired a cog-
nomen, was on the spot named *Gilpin*, amid
shouts that made the lonely valley ring.

We had now to cross a broad and rather rapid

rivulet, which flows from a lake of considerable
size, and winding through the glen, and then over
a wide and beautiful sand, falls into the sea at
the northern inlet, whither we were bound.
Having forded this stream where it is most shallow, we ascended the steep and rugged banks on
the farther side.   From the narrowness of the
path, it was now found necessary to proceed in
Indian file; and still more necessary, for safety sake,
to resign to the untamed spirit of *Gilpin*, the honour
of leading the way.   Indeed this was a distinction
he insisted upon claiming on all occasions; consequently he was always getting into trouble; and
then, when taking the wrong direction, no sooner
was he aware that others, by following a more
direct course, had got before him, than he started
off at full speed, over any and every obstacle that
obstructed his way, till he had overtaken and distanced the rest.   The struggle for precedence in
this ambitious youngster was a constant source of
merriment during our ride.

We had now reached a cultivated and fertile
hamlet.   It is sheltered by two lofty promontories,
between which there runs, for several miles into
the land, from the North Atlantic, a narrow frith
or *voe*.   To the west, the cottages are scattered on
the hillside, and the banks, clothed with wild rose-
bushes, honeysuckle, and ferns, slope steeply to the
water's edge.   This snug picturesque hamlet contains a population of above a hundred.   A pleasing
object in a locality so remote, is a neat school-
house, recently erected by the owner of the land.

The soil here is sandy and warm, so that *malgré* its hyperborean situation, the crops are generally more productive and sooner ripe, than in almost any other district of the Islands. Beyond the cottages stretches the promontory of Hermaness, terminating in a bluff headland. On the eastern side of the frith, there are no dwellings, or signs of cultivation; a still higher promontory, with most precipitous cliffs, covered with sea-fowl, being all that greets the eye, and this place is called *Saxa Frith.* *Herman* and *Saxa,* be it known, were the names of two renowned giants of the olden time, one of whom threw a stone in great wrath at the other, which, however, fell short, and still remains a sunken rock in the middle of the frith; whereat, as may be supposed, the giant adversary chuckled greatly. On both sides of the frith the precipices are indented by deep gullies and geos, and also by caverns, some of which have splendid arches.

In these caverns dwells the great seal, and we hoped, in the course of our day's excursion, to kill or capture one or more, if possible, of these noble denizens of the rocks and deep. We rode to the most northerly cottage in Great Britain, where there is a fishing-station, at which the boats deliver to the curer their newly caught fish. These are immediately salted, and afterwards dried on a stony beach, and thus prepared for the market.

We found two commodious six-oared boats awaiting us, and immediately embarked on the marine part of our expedition.

We proceeded first, round the north-west point,

exploring several caverns and geos, admiring their endlessly varied forms and sizes, but without finding any indications of seals. Once, indeed, by the aid of a perspective glass, we saw several, reposing on some low rocks, and apparently unaware of our vicinity. We immediately took measures to approach them stealthily, but a flock of herring-gulls being on the *out-look*, and aware of the danger, dashed down among the seals with vociferous cries, so that the latter instantly plunged into the water and disappeared. As we proceeded, the scenery became still more varied and sublime. Rugged precipices frowned overhead, down which tumbled the mountain-rill, like a glittering cord. The numerous detached rocks of the most fantastic shapes, among which we threaded our watery way, were covered with thousands of screaming seafowl; and the mighty majestic ocean stretched far away, northwards and westwards, in illimitable expanse, gleaming under the beams of an unclouded sun.

Nature in her wildest moods here reigns in the glory of unbroken solitude, so far at least as man, with his turmoil, is concerned; and it is in such a scene, that a devout mind perhaps best loves to hold communion with his Creator, surrounded only by *His* workmanship. On the present occasion, these natural sentiments were heightened by the indulgence of the most delightful social sympathies; what wonder if we were all full of enthusiasm?

Having continued our course westward, as far as we considered our time would permit, we sought

among the rocks a suitable place to land; and ere
long entering a circuitous opening, reached a flat
rock, the size of a spacious dining-room; here,
under the grateful shelter of an overhanging cliff,
and surrounded by myriads of busy sea-fowl, we
refreshed ourselves with the substantial fare we
had brought with us. We then returned to the
northern point, near which lies the group of islets,
called "The Burrafrith Sherries," affording pasture to five or six sheep only, and on which it is
very frequently impossible to effect a landing. On
this day, however, *Old Ocean* was particularly com-
plaisant, and allowed us to land, and gather shell-
fish and bits of stone, as trophies from the domains
where he usually reigns "alone in his glory."
We were exceedingly anxious after this, to reach
an insulated rock, the most northerly spot belonging to the British Islands. It is called the *Utsta*,
or *Outstack*, and at a little distance looks very
like a gigantic sea-horse. It affords shelter not
even for a sheep; indeed in violent storms the
wild Atlantic waves not unfrequently pass right
over it.

We approached the rock very warily for we
hoped to find some seals sunning themselves in
that lonely retreat. We were not disappointed,
for one of our number who scrambled up, and
peeped cautiously over the top, saw two large seals
close to the edge of the water, and could even hear
them singing to each other, in their own peculiar
cooing plaintive tones, expressive of ease and enjoy-

ment. The sportsman instantly retreated, and enjoining strict silence, crept on his hands and knees round the rock, till he succeeded in getting within range of the unsuspecting seals, and taking aim at the male over an intervening point. The report was soon heard, when a fine Newfoundland dog which accompanied us, bounded from the man that held him, with a joyful yell, and we all scrambled out of the boats to reach the scene. The poor seal lay dead, having been shot with a small single bullet right through the brain. We saw his mate no more; but she continued to haunt the fatal spot, and was killed by the same hand a few days afterwards. We now, with some considerable difficulty, bagged our noble game, which was above eight feet long, and almost black from great age. It yielded fourteen gallons of oil, and weighed six hundred weight.

Crossing the mouth of the frith, which is not above half-a-mile in width, we came to the base of the highest precipice, that of Saxafrith, 800 feet in perpendicular height. The face of the rock is covered with innumerable birds, all in a very restless and excited state at this time, as the young ones were fledged; and it was curious and interesting to see them essaying their first flights, under the parent care, preparatory to their speedy migration.

We then proceeded through a majestic archway, leading from the north-east point of the promontory into the frith. It is several hundred feet long, and in some places one hundred high, variegated on the roof and sides with a thousand delicate shades of colouring. Here the tones of a flute awoke the sweetest echoes; and the report of a fowling-piece reverberated in sounds absolutely deafening.

We now proceeded homewards, along the precipitous cliffs of the eastern side of the frith, stopping occasionally to allow the younger sportsmen to improve their skill, till the eager hands had half filled the boats with the various birds that frequent such localities,—guillimots, razor-bills, oyster-catchers, cormorants, puffins, and gulls of various species, and above all, the beautiful and gentle kittiwake. All these sea-fowl the boatmen accepted as excellent eating.

The sun was sinking amidst clouds of crimson and gold, as we reached the landing-place. The boats had returned from their previous night's fishing, deeply laden; and we found a busy and exciting scene at the beach, from which, however, we hastened away to partake of the grateful refreshment of potent and excellent tea, which awaited us at the cottage of the factor, or superintendant of the station.

Rested and invigorated, we strolled along the romantic pathway overhanging the cliff, to our ponies, which were tethered and grazing on the sloping bank. More sober and subdued, but equally delightful, was our homeward ride, as we chatted over our *adventures;* and we reached our dwel-

ling when it was nearly dark, after spending a
day which no cloud, either on our minds, or on
the face of nature had for an instant obscured,—
one of those that remain in long after years to
the chastened spirit, a "green spot in memory's
waste."

CHAPTER IX.

OLE OLAFSON.

A SHETLAND TALE OF OTHER TIMES.

ABOUT the year 1793, during the American war, most of the inhabitants of the town of Lerwick were gazing with intense interest on two vessels, which unexpectedly appeared in the south entrance of Bressa Sound. The wind was light and contrary, and the ships were beating up for the anchorage so slowly, as to keep the spectators in a complete furnace of curiosity and suspense, it might be, in some minds, even of fear; for one of the vessels was a frigate, too probably belonging to our enemies. At all events, it was none of the British cruisers that occasionally called at the islands. It must be confessed, the Lerwegians had little cause to feel confidence in the guns of their small battery. Had there been any object to be gained by the exploit, the cannon of one frigate could soon have silenced Fort-Charlotte; but in truth, the poverty and obscurity of Shetland were its best defences in those disastrous times.

The Lerwick people were quite accustomed to the arrival of ships from many parts of the world, seldom indeed for trade, as now, but they often

sought shelter there, from the war of nations, or
the scarcely less dreaded war of elements; or
they came for supplies of stores or water; or perchance they sought privacy for smuggling. But
the spectators saw no probability that the stranger
vessels belonged to any of these classes. No wonder that anxiety increased as they approached.
At last some one said, "Let us go to Robbie
Hunt, he will perhaps know them."

Robbie was a lad of weak intellect, who, however, had a tact or faculty so surprising, for recog-
nizing the *physiognomy* of ships, that he could at a
glance tell, not only every man-of-war accustomed
to visit Bressa Sound, and all the traders from
Leith or Hamburgh, resorting there, but every
sail he had seen, of whatever rig or tonnage, including hundreds of Dutch herring-fishers, and
fleets of Greenland whalers.

He was standing apart on a little eminence
above the town, and he too was staring at the
ships.

"What can yonder vessels be, Robbie, lad?"
said the interrogator.

"Oh, the foremost is the *Marianne of Hull*, the
Greenland whaler."

"What, that fine sailer!—that rakish-looking
beauty, a blubber whaler! Robbie, you are wrong
for once."

"Hoot, not I," said Robbie; "she was here last
year to join the convoy. She had been a French
privateer, and Captain Olafson, our ain countryman, ye ken, got her for the Greenland trade."

" Robbie is right," said one of the persons now clustering round the ship oracle; " the *Marianne* is a fine vessel, and Olè Olafson knows how to handle her; and see, he is hoisting his colours, one after the other."

" Wad ye just len' us the glass, Maister?" respectfully asked poor Robbie of the gentleman, who was peering through a pocket telescope.

It was a short but sufficient survey Robbie took, when shutting the glass carefully, and with an evident feeling of devout admiration of its powers, he pronounced authoritatively it was none other than the *Marianne* having charge of a French prize. " For," said he, " the frigate has the Frenchie's colours lowered, and the British Jack flying above them."

" Ah, Robbie lad," said the owner of the perspective glass, fired with enthusiasm for his country's glory, " if what thou says be true, thou shall have for an awmous* that glass thou looks at so wistfully."

" That wad be an awmous indeed," said the lad, his usually unsettled eye sparkling with joy and confidence. " I may think it for my ain already," and he reluctantly resigned it to the less sanguine proprietor.

Next day Robbie called the telescope his own; perhaps the only thing in this world his wishes had ever hovered round. Henceforward the poor

---

* *Awmous*—corruption of *alms*—a gift in charity; but more usually in payment of a vow.

harmless being had an assistant and a friend—a
silent one indeed, but tenderly cherished—adapted
to the only pursuit (if it may be so called) his intellect seemed capable of grasping. Hours together he would sit gazing at the shipping, till
every rope and block became as familiar as the
cut of the sails, and the turn of the hulls, had formerly been. Robbie lived to a good old age,—
kindly treated by his countrymen,—but he is now
gathered to his fathers.

Our main object, however, was to relate, not his
history, but the daring and gallant exploit by which
a fine French frigate was indeed captured and
brought to Bressa Sound by a Greenland whaler.

During the war the fleet of vessels destined for
the whaling grounds of the icy sea, generally
rendezvous-ed in Shetland, and there met a man-of-
war convoy. Before this precaution was adopted,
French and American privateers had committed
great depredations on the imperfectly armed, and
still less-disciplined whalers, tearing from them by
violence and blood-shed, their hardly won cargoes
of blubber,—sinking the vessels, and bearing the
crews to a foreign prison,—such is the reckless
cruelty of WAR!

In the spring of the year we have mentioned,
however, the ships sailed for the North *without* a
convoy. Whether they had missed her, or it was
in sheer fool-hardiness does not clearly appear.
The vessels were armed in such fashion as merchantmen usually were in those days; only one or
two of the number having been originally destined

for, or employed in a different service, were rather
more efficiently furnished with guns, and of these
was the "Marianne of Hull." Her captain was
Olè Olafson, a stout-hearted Shetlander, worthy of
a nobler command.

On the 6th of June the fleet of vessels were
scattered about near the margin of the ice expecting whales, but in each a watch was appoiuted to
look out for suspicious looking vessels, and also to
keep sight of their companion ships.

The weather was lovely. The sun kept running
his cloudless courses, almost in a circle, for his disk
hardly dipped beneath the horizon of icebergs, ere
he rose again, shedding full effulgence on the purity
of the icicles, till they reflected all the colours of
the rainbow in dazzling brilliancy. About noon,
one of the outermost vessels showed signals of
alarm, and hastened to join the main body of the
fleet, where all the other ships also speedily con-
gregated, not unlike a herd of startled sheep. It
was soon perceived, that a hostile sail was bearing
down upon them,—to continue the metaphor, like
a wolf ready to pounce on the timid and defenceless
flock. The enemy doubtless expected he should
find the fold unguarded, and gather, as he had
done before, a rich and easy prey. The whaling
ship-masters now held a council of war. After a
marvellously short consultation they agreed unani-
mously as to their tactics, which were, to keep as
close as possible,—push forward to meet the foe,
and if he attempted hostilities, the whole fleet were
to give him battle simultaneously. This was cer-

tainly the most politic course, as it was the most characteristic of British sailors. These hardy men shook hands in ratification of their treaty of amity and aid, while the crews afterwards responded to the resolution with eager acclamations.

The fleet, therefore, made immediate sail towards the Frenchman, who never doubting, from their dauntless approach, so unlike their behaviour on other occasions, when they had no such spirit as Olafson's presiding at their councils, that they had an armed convoy to protect them, at first slackened sail, then seemed to waver for a little, and finally set off on an opposite tack.

One or two of the best sailing Greenlandmen gave the enemy chase in good style, by way of driving him out of their neighbourhood; and the " Marianne," being by far the fleetest, soon distanced all her friends. Her gallant commander, in the ardour of pursuit, forgot, or if he remembered, disregarded the compact that the British vessels were to keep close company. The chase, on the other hand, was confirmed in his belief that his pursuer was a man-of-war of force far superior to his own, and seized with a panic, he began to throw his guns overboard to lighten his ship, hoping thus to baffle the utmost speed of the " Marianne."

For a time his vessel's speed equalled his expectations; but a slight change in the wind gave the whaler an advantage so great, that it was evident she was rapidly nearing the frigate. Captain Olafson now called his men together, and in a pithy speech told them, " he was resolved to capture or sink the lubberly Frenchman who had shown the white feather, and durst not fight without his guns." A shout of acquiescence told him he had bold hearts to stand by him; so setting every stitch of canvas, Olafson gained fast on the foe. Life and death seemed in the chase; the two vessels were soon out of sight of all the other whalers, and the " Marianne" at length came within hailing distance of the Frenchman. Leaping into the fore-rigging of his ship, Captain Olafson shouted through his trumpet to the enemy, ordering him to "strike his colours instantly."

" To whom ?" asked the French captain, feeling himself at the mercy of a gigantic foe, whose high bulwarks and cannon mouths, more than half of them, however, being only painted ones, looked sufficiently formidable.

" To the Marianne whaler of Hull," was the bold reply. " Strike your colours, or I'll sink you," and a shot of defiance boomed over the water.

The Frenchman now found how he had suffered himself to be deceived. He had sacrificed almost all his guns, and his men cowed and crouching, besought him to surrender at discretion. Captain Olafson went on board immediately, with a party of men well-armed, and on their guard, as he was not without a suspicion the enemy had made a feint to entrap him. Of this, however, they had no intention, under the cannon mouth as they were. They were quickly deprived of their re-

maining arms, and afterwards dispersed as prisoners among the other whalers. A prize crew
was put on board the frigate, and Captain Olafson
made sail for the Shetlands. On the eighth day he
brought his prize into Bressa Sound in triumph,
as we have described; and for this gallant exploit
he received from his countrymen all *they* had to
give,—the honest meed of their praise,—and from
his country's rulers, the cold one of *thanks*.

CHAPTER X.

THE SMUGGLERS.

ANOTHER STORY OF OLDEN TIME.

A FEW years ago a young clergyman was paying a short visit to a friend in the country,
the widow of a naval officer recently deceased.
He found the family much affected by the apparently approaching end of a faithful and attached de-
pendant rather than servant of the household, an
aged negro, who had been bequeathed to their
friendship and protection by a much valued relative.

The clergyman, at the request of his hostess,
repaired to the chamber where lay the dying
African, far from his native land indeed, but surrounded by the comforts of civilization, and the
consolations of religion. In reply to the words of
hope held out to him by the minister, he replied,—
" Yes, I go to Massa." A bright smile played on
his face, and again murmuring, "Massa," he sunk
to everlasting rest, one more example added to
the many we have seen in the despised race of
Africa, of fidelity and attachment, strong even in
death. The negro was laid, as he had requested,
near to his deceased master, to whom he had been

so fondly attached, who had indeed rescued him
from the most degraded and wretched slavery, and
introduced him into the glorious freedom of Chris-
tianity.   The most important of his worldly effects
were a few books and papers.   Among the latter
was his *will*, wherein he bequeathed the not incon-
siderable savings of his wages, one-half to the
African Association, and the other to the youngest
daughter of his widowed mistress.   The following
narrative, drawn up, it would appear, by his former
master, and in which mention is made of the faithful Mungo himself, was found carefully tied up by
itself, apparently a hoarded relic of one to whom
he was under the holiest obligations.   We now
present it to the reader as illustrative of the manners of the Shetlanders at the date of the story,
and as one among many interesting incidents that
took place under a state of society unique at the
time in Britain, but long since passed away :—

JANUARY, 1825.

TOWARDS the close of the last century I had returned to my native land with an independent for-
tune ; but where were the friends of my youth to
share it with me ?—and with a constitution sorely
shaken by the sultry winds of India, and the death-
dealing plague of Egypt.   Yet was I not too far advanced in the journey of life to feel at liberty to
neglect what health and strength still remained ;
so I resolved to try for a season, if the bracing and
equable climate of a more northern region would
infuse aught of vigour into my frame, or change

of scene chase away the sadness which too often pressed heavily on my heart. With this object in view, I was roused one lovely morning in the latter end of June, by my servant, a simple-minded affectionate negro, who informed me, " the captain was below." I felt more than half inclined to resist the summons, and court again the dreamy slumber. " I think I shan't go after all, Mungo," said I.

" As Massa pleases. Berry cold I s'pose north dere ;" and the poor fellow shivered by anticipation at the thought.

But smiling at honest Mungo, and my own momentary indecision, I started up, and was soon ready for my voyage, and in presence of the captain, a staunch old Greenland seaman. " Is the wind fair?" was my first hurried question.

" Fair to be sure. Look alive ; here is Ned at the door for your traps." Mungo looked quite resigned, his will at all times being that of his master, and though the accommodations on board of a trading vessel were not so sumptuous then as they are now, in the noble steamers of our coasts, I made myself as comfortable as circumstances permitted, gave way to the joyous buoyancy inspired by the balmy sea breezes, and in four days, so prosperous was our voyage, we entered the Bay of Lerwick, the solitary town of the far-north Shetlands. Here the sight was a most exhilarating one, as we came in before a stiff breeze. A great number of Dutch vessels, engaged in the early herring-fishing, with many other ships of different nations lay in the

spacious natural harbour. A corvette protecting
the foreign fishers, and watching their proceedings,
and a frigate, at whose taffrail floated " the meteor
flag of England," were most conspicuous. A
beautiful little cutter also attracted my attention ;
she was employed in the prevention of the smuggling trade, for which these islands, in their remoteness and privacy, and the number and excel-
lence of their harbours, afforded many facilities. The
bay of Bressa Sound is completely land-locked,
the island which gives it its name stretching across
the entrance, and leaving to the north and south
navigable inlets flanked by bold and precipitous
headlands. The little fishing-town of Lerwick is
built on a rather steep acclivity, and looked snug
and neat. On landing, however, the scene was by
no means so agreeable. The streets are narrow
and confined; and neither the town, nor its en-
virons present any objects calculated to interest a
stranger. Resisting, therefore, the exuberant and
primitive hospitality, which was proffered me on
every hand, I was anxious to hurry off, panting
for the quiet and seclusion which had now become
most congenial to me. By the good offices of
one of the respectable inhabitants of Lerwick, I
soon succeeded in engaging a large boat, and six
rowers, to convey me to one of the more distant
islands, to whose sole proprietor I had letters of
introduction. As I stood on the quay, preparing
to depart, I could not help admiring the beautiful
symmetry of my passage-boat. The Shetland
boats are built after the fashion of the classic Nor-

wegian yawl, pointed fore and aft; they carry one large square-sail, and when well managed, are considered not only the most graceful, but the safest description of boats of their size with which we are acquainted.

It was evening when we rowed swiftly out of the bay. The westerly breeze had settled down into a perfect calm, and I thought in all my wanderings I had never witnessed a more lovely scene. Indeed nothing can be more exquisitely soothing and delightful, than a mid-summer night on the water, among those lonely Isles. The sea was smooth as glass; the shores of the larger islands were rocky and precipitous, and inland stretched a long line of bleak and treeless hills; but we were threading our way through innumerable green islets, and detached rocks, rising out of the sleeping ocean, like giant relics of a former world. The glass-like mirror reflected the high banks, and their deepening shadows, and the stillness was broken only by the occasional shrill scream of a seabird, and the measured stroke of the supple oar, as we glided along, often only a few feet from the rocky bank or overhanging cliff. At length the sun sank below the horizon, but the soft twilight lingered, till his rising beams again illuminated the glorious expanse of ocean, now stretching in illimitable grandeur before us. I shall never forget the enchanting sweet tranquillity of that night, and voyage among the Shetland Isles.

Two individuals by my side, however, were more disposed to yield to the sleepy, than to the

poetical influences of the hour, I mean Mungo,
and my noble Newfoundland dog Neptune. With
a companion like the latter, to whom one can com-
plain when melancholy, caress when joyous, and
storm at when vexed; and with an attendant, like
my faithful negro, ever on the alert when *Massa*
calls, and whom no indulgence or familiarity can
cause to forget the distance and respect he considers due, a man may travel the world over, and
be nearly independent of other society.

I reached the residence of Mr Rendale about
breakfast-time, and was received in the spirit of
genuine northern hospitality, the warmth of the
welcome making ample amends for the coldness of
the climate. I was shown into the apartment
where the family were assembled for their morning
meal. Presently my letters of introduction were
placed, without being opened, or even looked at,
on the mantel-piece, and I was grasped by a
friendly hand, and at once seated at the hospitable
board, simply because I was a stranger.   Yes,
kind and hospitable Islanders, the blessing of many
a stranger and voyager lingers around your simple,
happy hearths!—and not the least heartfelt ac-
knowledgment is here registered.   The mansion of
Mr Rendale was situated on the inland shores of a
small sheltered bay, open, however, in one direction
to the fury of the Atlantic; and it was fearfully
sublime in a storm from the west, to see the majestic waves come sweeping, in one unbroken swell,
even to the base of the rocky eminence on which the
house was built.   The *laird* was an elderly man,

whose pleasing and gentlemanly manners were
rather at variance with an eccentric exterior. He
was upwards of six feet high, gaunt and thin, but
extremely active and strong. His yellow locks,
very slightly tinged with gray, floated on his
shoulders, and together with his pale but keen blue
eyes, sufficiently bespoke his Scandinavian origin.
In his deportment a stranger might soon detect,
mingled with suavity and kindness, a slightly self-
satisfied air of importance and ease, the result of
a life spent among his dependants, and inferiors in
rank and education, and in the peace and abundance of a patrimonial inheritance. His servants
and tenants loved and respected him, and did his
bidding at all times with cheerfulness, as indeed
his liberality and indulgence amply merited. One
important personage in his household, alone, invariably took his own way, whether it were his
master's or not,—this was the laird's *factotum*, to
whom I was early introduced in due form. He
was head-bailiff, superintendent, fish-curer, clerk,
storekeeper, and twenty other things besides; of
middle age, stout, and athletic, and indefatigably
active. He was absolutely necessary to the con-
ducting of the multitudinous affairs pertaining to a
Shetland proprietorship; and with the greatest
apparent deference and respect to all his master's
wishes, and an unhesitating assent to all his opinions, he yet contrived to do most things after his
own fashion, and in his own time.

Mr Rendale's family consisted only of a son and
daughter. The former was a fine spirited young

man, who would rather have roved over the world
than be imprisoned in an island of Shetland; but
his father's hopes were centred in him, and he had
become necessary to the old man as an assistant
and companion. Young Rendale was delighted at
my arrival, and though I was many years his
senior, we were quickly on a footing of perfect in-
timacy; the merits and capabilities of my rifle and
dog, being as so many passports to the familiarity
of old acquaintanceship.

The daughter, Mary Rendale, was a sweet girl,
in her twentieth year; she was very fair like her
father, and their gothic ancestors; her eyes were
of that changeful shade of grey, that would sometimes cause the gazer to believe them black; and
they were shaded by long thick lashes, hiding,
while they created the fluctuating expression which
betokens softness and sensibility; her voice was
melodious, yet plaintive, and her manner was
graceful, gentle, and unaffected, combining a lady-
like self-possession, with a kindly frankness, such
as I never witnessed in greater perfection than in
this interesting Shetland maiden.

On the morning of my arrival, having finished
our protracted breakfast, Miss Rendale had left us
for the performance of her household duties, and
we were deeply engaged planning and discussing
various pleasure excursions, when two strangers
were shown into the apartment. One was a coarse
ruffianly looking man, evidently a foreigner, yet
speaking English fluently, though not correctly.
His face was large and red, his eyes fiery and

bloodshot, glancing with a quick, restless, and suspicious expression; he was clad in a common seaman's dress, but a valuable ring glittered on his finger. His companion presented a singular contrast. He was a slight-made but strongly knit young Englishman; his face and figure were extremely handsome, and his age apparently about twenty-four. His dress likewise was that of a seaman, but of finer materials than his companion's, displaying to great advantage an agile and finely proportioned frame. The former of these strangers was captain, the latter second in command, of a Dutch vessel, which lay snugly moored in a small creek near the mansion-house, and whose masts were visible from where we sat. The strangers had received some kindly attentions from Mr Rendale, and were now come to take leave. The young lieutenant's eyes wandered anxiously round for a few moments, but apparently not finding what they sought, he hastily rose and left the room. The captain often glanced uneasily at me, and was reserved and morose. From his appearance, I should have supposed him daring and desperate, as indeed it proved, for his vessel was engaged in the smuggling trade. After a short interval, we accompanied him to the sea-side, where he was in a few minutes joined by his lieutenant, and in a very short time their vessel was under weigh. Was it but a fancy of my own that Mary looked paler at dinner, and more pensive in her demeanour than usual? Could it be that this gentle and lovely girl, had linked her affections with

one engaged in an illegal and dangerous traffic?—
for so much I understood thus early of the history
of the strangers, not indeed from my host himself,
who, though doubtless, aware of the real character
of his late guests, perhaps from the frequency of
smuggling, considered it but a trifling offence.

The same night I was aroused from a heavy
dreamless sleep, by the impatient growling of
Neptune. My efforts to quiet him proving unavailing, I jumped up, and went to the window.
In the twilight of the summer midnight I perceived several men coming towards the house from
the landing-place or low pier, towards which I
looked. They appeared to be fishermen returning
from sea; but lingering a moment to gaze again
on the wild sequestered scenery, I observed, that
the men carried bags and small casks, and that
they were met with a stealthy gesture of caution
by the laird's *major-domo*. He glanced upwards to
my window, but I stood in the shadow, until I
had seen a boat put off from the land, and row
swiftly out of the bay, when not choosing to play
the spy on any of the doings of the household of
my hospitable friend, I retired to my couch, having
by my cursory inspection satisfied Neptune that I
was on the alert. Thrusting his nose into my
hand for the expected caress in reward for his
watchfulness, my faithful attendant responded to
my " All right boy!" by a low whine of satisfaction, and resigned himself, like his master, to repose. I did not think fit to mention this slight
interruption of my rest to my host, or any of his

family, and the circumstance had nearly passed from my mind, when subsequent events recalled it.

A few days now passed swiftly and pleasantly away. I seemed to inhale new life with the pure invigorating sea breezes, and simple fare of Shetland. In the peaceful yet cheerful occupations of their fisheries and their farms, and the onerous but honourable duties of the laird towards his numerous tenantry, I soon saw reasons which made me cease to wonder that the Shetlanders prefer the iron-bound shores, and bleak hills, of their rocky fatherland, to all the world beside! On the fifth day, as we sat at an early dinner, Magnus, the laird's *factotum* entered hastily, saying, " A sail coming in, sir." We turned our eyes to the window, from which we had a view of the bay, and Mr Rendale seized his telescope. After a momentary glance, he exclaimed, " What brings the fellow back this way ?" Mary started, and changed colour, and in another moment her father cried, " A tall mast over the land's point! A cutter that is, surely, Magnus ?" shutting his glass with a vehement gesture, and apparently stung with anxiety, " Poor fellow, he is chased, without doubt." And so it proved. The cutter I had seen in Bressa Sound had got intelligence of the smuggler by means of the very boatmen who had come with me, had chased him through the island channels, till finding he could no longer hope to escape, he ran in here, and turned to bay.

" Will he fight, father, think you ?" cried young

Rendale, while Mary shivered and trembled under the excess of her agitation. But hardly had the words escaped him, when the signal-gun to yield was answered by one of defiance. The conflict was, however, very short, though the smuggler fought desperately. Seeing the overpowering emotion of Miss Rendale, I caused the housekeeper to be summoned, to whose care I consigned her. Mr Rendale, and his son, with generous enthusiasm thought only of their late acquaintances, now evidently in the clutches of the coast-guard cruiser; but the *major-domo* was in such a paroxysm of excitement, that considering what I had been an involuntary witness of, the second night of my sojourn, I suspected he had anxieties of his own, of which his master and family were profoundly ignorant.

Shortly after the firing had ceased, a boat was seen approaching the shore from the cutter, and her commander, Lieutenant Harding, called on Mr Rendale. He was a young and good looking man, but he conducted himself with stiffness and hauteur, as if willing to let it be seen he was armed with authority, and triumphant in its exercise. " I have taken the Dutch smuggler, sir," he said. " Her commander is killed, and I have his lieutenant in custody on a charge of murder ;" and a withering sneer crossed his countenance as he uttered the word.

" Murder ! Alas, alas !" exclaimed the worthy Rendale.

" Murder !" echoed his son.

" Murder! I hope not," said I.

" Yes, gentlemen, I spoke advisedly. I saw the young man pistol one of my men in the exercise of his duty, and he is since dead. I sail immediately," he continued, as we stood aghast at the serious aspect of affairs; " and probably, Mr Rendale, your evidence may be required as to what you know of this spark, who, if I mistake not is a friend of yours."

" We have been interested in him certainly," promptly replied my excellent host. " He is an Englishman, and a gentleman; and I trust he will be acquitted of this very serious charge."

" We shall see that, by-and-by," responded Harding; " meanwhile I have the honour to wish you a good afternoon."

When he was gone, I frankly expressed my dislike of his bearing, and then I learned various circumstances which confirmed the unpleasing impression. It appeared that he had frequently visited Mr Rendale before, in the course of his cruises on duty, and had even paid his addresses to Mary, who repelled them; when, hearing from some spy in his service, of the attentions of his present unfortunate prisoner, jealousy sharpened his zeal in his official duty, and led to the chase and capture of the Dutch smuggler. Hasty and deeply anxious was now our consultation. I sympathized warmly in the feelings of the family of Mr Rendale, and felt that indirectly I had been the cause of the present untoward occurrence. My Shetland host had few friends and little interest,

beyond the limits of his native isles, and it was
with ardent expressions of gratitude, that he heard
and accepted of my offer to follow at once the cutter, and exert all my good offices, and not trifling
influence, on behalf of the young man, in whose
fate I was so suddenly and strangely interested.
A six-oared boat was therefore ordered to be got
ready immediately. Young Rendale insisted on
accompanying me; and it was hoped, that the
immediate object of our voyage would be mistaken
for the ordinary departure of a temporary guest.
In little more than a couple of hours I was told all
was prepared for our departure, and Mary sent a
request to see me. On repairing to the drawing-
room, where I found my interesting friend, I was
deeply moved by the expression of her fair face.
For some moments her emotion would not allow
of speech, but the frank and confiding grasp with
which she received my extended hand, told more
than words could have done. I felt a momentary
embarrassment, and hesitated in what terms I
might best and most delicately make known my
sympathy with her too evident concern at the unfortunate events which had occurred; but with the
native tact of womanly frankness and dignity, re-
covering herself, she expressed at once what she
wished to communicate. " I trust I need not assure you of the high sense I entertain of the proof
of friendship you are giving us; but it is right I
should inform you of circumstances relating to
him in whom you are so kindly interested, which I
only can." She grew very pale as she proceeded.

" He is placed in a peculiarly cruel and dangerous
position, and I feel that I am mainly the cause. I
will speak to you unreservedly, for I know you
appreciate my motives. He is of a highly respectable English family, and in consequence of some
youthful indiscretion, left his home when yet a
boy, to which, having heard of the death of his
parents, he never returned. Having an ardent
predilection for the navy, he entered that service
as a common seaman. It would be wasting too
much of that time, every moment of which is now
so precious, were I to detail by what steps he even-
tually found a situation more fitted to his birth
and education, on board a Dutch corvette. At
Lerwick, two years ago, I first met him. The
same reckless imprudence, that led him to take
the first hasty step, dictated the still more unguarded one, that he might have opportunities
of coming here, of accepting a berth on board the
schooner, Goedvrow, with whose real character
he was at first unacquainted. Oh to what fearful
consequences has this led! Lieutenant Harding
had endeavoured to fasten a quarrel on him, when
they first met at Lerwick, and ever since has pursued him with unrelenting animosity, and I feel
assured will persecute him even to death." She
shuddered, and grew still paler, yet maintained
admirable composure and self-possession. Thus
it is, we often find that in the greatest emer-
gencies, the energies of a gentle, sensitive female,
show her to be equal to any task however trying,
that her duty or her affections may impose on her.

I asked some further necessary questions for my direction.

"And his name, Miss Rendale? I have only heard it cursorily, and did not attend to it."

"Edward Brookes," she faintly replied, "is his *real* name;" and her agitation was no longer all her own.

"What do you say?" exclaimed I. "Brookes is the name of one of the branches of my family; and Edward—poor Edward—the noble, but wayward boy, can it possibly be he?"

A few words more, and I became nearly convinced, that the unhappy lover of Mary Rendale, was indeed the only and orphan son of my eldest sister, for whom, I had for years, and in every country, sought sorrowing, and whose discovery, under almost any circumstances, I thought I should have hailed with rapture. He was the only relative I now had on earth,—the only heir I could hope to find for my dearly-bought wealth; but a prisoner,—a felon, under the charge of murder! For this I was indeed unprepared. Stung with contending emotions, I now hastened to take leave of Miss Rendale. I pressed her hand to my lips, and suppressing my own bursting feelings, I endeavoured cheerfully to assure her of my indefatigable exertions, and my sanguine hopes of success on behalf of the ardent and rash, but noble youth.

Behold me again threading my midnight watery way among the Shetland Isles; but not the calm beauty of my late voyage was half so delightful as was now, the stiff favouring breeze which filled

the sail of our canoe-like boat, swiftly impelling us
on our errand of friendship and mercy. Arrived
at Lerwick, we were so fortunate as to find a
coasting vessel about to sail for the Orkneys, and
in her we obtained a passage. In two days more
we found ourselves pursuing our route as rapidly
as a post-chaise and four could carry us. The
cutter with her prize and prisoner was, however,
in Leith before us, but I soon obtained access to the
accused.

How eagerly I scanned his noble but dejected
countenance. There were, indeed, the bright
hazel eye, and the curling auburn locks; but the
answers to my two breathless questions would have
sufficed. The name of his paternal home, and of
his *father's sister*, thrilled with magic force to my
heart, like a native melody long unheard, and
dearly loved; for they spoke of my birth-place
and friends, and of my first—my only—my lament-
ed love. Oh with what sensations did I behold
him wounded and a prisoner! I soon learned, as
indeed I had all along suspected, that the charge
of murder was utterly false, and invented by his
enemy, to involve him in danger and disgrace, and if
possible alienate from him the heart Harding coveted
to make his own. Edward informed me that his
pistol had indeed gone off in the *melée* of boarding,
but had injured no one, and that the man the lieutenant asserted he had shot, had been killed a few
minutes afterwards by the captain of the smuggler. "And he alas is dead too," said the unhappy young man, wringing his hands; "and I

must die an ignominious death. But"—he added after a pause, his eyes gleaming with a fearful and almost insane wildness,—" he is doomed also. Eight of the surviving crew have sworn that he shall die. By flood and field—by hill and by dale—in the house or homestead—by night and by day—he will be tracked with the same deathless vengeance of the untiring slot-hound, with which he has persecuted me." His form dilated and quivered with fury, as he quoted the terrible words of the oath of vengeance sworn by these desperate men.

I need hardly say I was not long absent from the cell of my unfortunate nephew, while young Rendale exerted the warmest devotion of friendship in the necessary details for the comfort and acquittal of the prisoner. By the assistance of an excellent clergyman, my poor Edward's mind was speedily brought into a more befitting frame; his frenzied deportment was hushed into the serenity of conscious innocence, and the noble youth, daily and hourly more endeared himself to my distracted heart. I early proposed to Edward, pursuant to Miss Rendale's desire, that I should write to request her presence in Edinburgh; but he said it would only increase their mutual affliction, and he had made her wretched enough already; yet could I see, that he was surprised and distressed at not hearing from her, and even clung, despite of himself, to the hope that she would have hastened to him unbidden. Oh how he wronged her by suspicions we did not dare to whisper to each other, while she was in reality exhausting every energy, in the means by which life and honour were to be procured for him to whom she had surrendered her heart, with all its tenderness and devotion. I did not fail to secure the most eminent counsel for my nephew's defence, but they gave me very little hope. The smuggling trade, they said, had been so openly and extensively pursued in Shetland, and the revenue-officers so often baffled and defied by both smugglers and natives, that they feared, even a recommendation to mercy, could it be procured, would be unavailing.

The lieutenant deponed on the prisoner's first examination, to his shooting the man, and if he persisted in his assertion, Edward must be condemned. Some dreary days and weeks now passed, during which I clung with increasing, yet hopeless affection to my late-found hapless relative. Four or five days previous to the one of trial, I observed, in the behaviour of Mr Gray, our worthy and able leading counsel, an unaccountable and joyous change, from blank hopelessness, to bursting excitement; yet when questioned, he shook his head despondingly as before. The eventful day at last arrived. Arraigned at the bar of his country, to be tried for his life, the gallant youth was graceful and composed, while I, as I stood by, might have been mistaken for the felon, so heavily did my affliction press upon me. The opening speech for the prosecution need not be repeated, though it struck ice-cold to my heart. Harding declared, that on the day named, the prisoner shot his coxwain while boarding the smuggling vessel. His cross-examination elicited nothing, and his withering glance at the accused, I shall never forget. When the evidence for the prosecution was closed, it seemed conclusive, and methought I read *guilty* in each juror's countenance. Mr Gray then rose. "What can he say to such evidence?" whispered my despairing heart.

He spoke a few sarcastic words, couched in a strain of caustic severity against Harding. "Gentlemen of the Jury," he concluded, "when you have heard the evidence I have to lead I shall leave my client's case in your hands with perfect confidence in your justice. Call in Frans Dekkel, formerly master of the Goedvrow of Amsterdam."

Edward started, and his frame shook, while his eye gleamed with hope. Harding became pale and livid, and Mr Gray turned to me with a triumphant gesture, as the identical Dutch captain I had seen in Shetland, and who was said to have been dead, entered the court. He was sorely changed by sickness, so that I could scarcely recognise him, yet he was collected and self-possessed.

" I object to that witness being sworn; he is a desperate character!" exclaimed the prosecutor.

" I beg your pardon, sir," said Mr Gray, "Mr Dekkel stands here a free man, and unaccused. I insist on his being sworn, my lord."

Dekkel was sworn, and stated, that *he* shot the man for whose death my nephew was arraigned. " I have been a reckless and lawless man," he said, " but I have been near to death, and I now freely confess my crime, that an innocent man may be saved!"

And for this it was, that Mary Rendale, instead of flying to her Edward's presence, had watched and nursed, with untiring self-devotion this unhappy outcast. Left for dead by his men, he was received into Mr Rendale's house by Magnus Ericson, who finding life yet remained, informed Miss Rendale, and was associated with her in the pious work of restoring the smuggler's health, and in so working on his mind, that as soon as practicable he came forward to save the innocent prisoner's life, by a frank avowal of the deed he had himself committed. The counsel for the prosecution failed not to take advantage of the circumstances in which Dekkel had been placed, to overthrow his evidence.

" This man's life has been spent," urged he, " in lawless adventure. He owes his preservation and recovery to the prisoner's friends; and moreover, how shall the single asseveration of such a character impeach, or even shake the evidence of Lieutenant Harding and his crew."

But for all these objections Mr Gray was happily prepared. By accident, he had discovered, that one of the cutter's crew was not forthcoming, and by the indefatigable, and almost incredible exertions of young Rendale, he had succeeded in tracing this man.

In the hospital of a remote town on the coast, where the cutter had called on her passage south, the seaman was found, suffering under a very slight

wound, and a course of active treatment, for what
in fact, required no treatment at all; and this the
purse of his commander had procured for him, in
order to keep him out of the way. Finally, then,
John Williams was called into Court, and with the
fearless frankness of an Englishman, and to the
unutterable discomfiture of Harding, he declared,
that he had seen the cutter's coxswain shot, not by
the accused, but by the last witness Dekkel; and,
moreover, that he had himself been bribed and
threatened, and finally incarcerated, to prevent
him giving his evidence.

As the reader will now anticipate, my nephew
was honourably acquitted, and on reaching my
lodgings, while, as yet, we could hardly realize our
happiness, so sudden and unlooked-for had been
the result, I placed in Edward's hands, as my first
welcome blessing, a letter from Mary, which he
read and re-read, and watered with his tears.
Young Rendale received, with an agitation that did
honour to his heart, the inarticulate murmurings
of Edward's gratitude, and informed us, that it was
considered necessary, to secure success, as well as to
keep the innocent prisoner's mind from the tortures
of suspense, carefully to conceal, until the moment
it was required, the existence of the evidence
which led to such a triumphant result. In the
happiness of that glad hour, honest Mungo, and
even Neptune, were permitted to participate.
Lieutenant Harding was indicted for perjury, but
escaped abroad, and has not since been heard of. I
eagerly exerted all my influence on behalf of poor

Frans Dekkel, but he lived not to profit by my success.

I obtained for Edward, at his urgent request, a commission in the British Navy, where he ably distinguished himself, while I re-purchased his patrimonial possessions, in the hope, that he would, ere long, share them with me, and at length succeed to them as his double inheritance.

Two years after the events I have narrated, I once again visited the Shetland Islands, when I received Mary Rendale as my niece; and she, and her family, are now the sweetest solace of my declining years.

CHAPTER XI.

THE FISHERMAN.

WILLIAM MANSON was a very affectionate husband and father, though the time as yet was short during which he had sustained these endearing relations; for he had but one child, who was hardly of an age to lisp his name. The summer of 1832 was very squally and unsettled; but, at length, in the end of July, a week of fine weather put all the fishermen on the alert, to seize the short favourable season that yet remained for their perilous vocation. The *rendezvous* of the fishing-boats is often at some miles distance from the mens' homes, and thither their wives, or sisters or daughters repair to meet them each morning on their return from the sea, to learn their welfare and success, to carry to them the little necessaries they require, and to take back some of the fish for the family's use. During the summer season, therefore, it is only Saturday afternoon and Sunday, or, as it is vernacularly called in the Norse, "*the helly*," that the fishermen enjoy the comforts and endearments of their homes.

Among those who were never absent to greet the return of the fishing-boats, was Jean, the wife of William Manson. She was very young, and a most gentle and interesting woman, devotedly attached to the companion of her life, who had been her early and only love.

It was on a very calm and lovely afternoon of the July I have mentioned, that all the boats, including that of William, took their accustomed way to the haff-fishing. Jean stood on the beach, with her eyes fixed on her husband's skiff, till it appeared but a speck on the ocean, and then, with a deep sigh, she turned her steps swiftly towards home, where she had left her child asleep in the care of a neighbour.

It was three in the morning, when all who had husbands, sons, or brothers, in those ill-fated little barks, were awaked by a violent storm; the sea rose in a manner so tumultuous and unexpected, that many persons thought it must have been caused by a submarine earthquake. By nine o'clock every cliff and beach whence a view of the far-stretching and troubled ocean could be obtained, was occupied by distracted females, looking for the barks which were never to return, and weeping in helpless, hopeless misery. Why repeat the too well known tale? Forty boats, with their hapless crews, being a third of the whole number, were swallowed up by the devouring waves.

William's boat was among the lost. It boots not now to tell the misery and desolation of so many hitherto happy hearths, or the hopes lingering in the mourners' hearts, which imaged forth many a dream, that some of the sufferers might have been picked up at sea, and would yet return. It was months ere those hopes were finally extinguished, and the bereaved ones learned to *feel* that they were indeed such.

The melancholy winter passed slowly away, and the month of March now arrived, when we shall take a peep at Jean's little cottage. She was seated at a cheerful fire. An infant two months old was asleep in the cradle which she rocked with her foot, while her other child was in bed close by. Her sister, some years older than herself, and an active, judicious, and affectionate woman, had just hung over the fire the small pot of potatoes for supper; and now seating herself with her knitting, looked long and anxiously in the fair but faded face of the young widow, who mechanically plied the accustomed knitting-needles, while a smothered sigh, and a bursting tear, told the anguished thoughts that occupied her mind.

" Jean, my woman," began, in accents of the deepest compassion and sympathy, the affectionate sister; then breathing a short prayer to heaven for fortitude, she proceeded in a more cheerful tone, as the poor widow raised her meek tearful eyes, and struggled for a smile of resignation,—" Jean, you have borne your affliction like a Christian, while you have felt it like a wife, and by the good help of God, you will not fail now to rouse yourself, and endeavour to do your duty to your helpless children; and only just think what a comfort they are, and will be to you. But you know, dear Jean, that the labouring season is now come, and

I ought to go to help our poor father and mother to get their voar* finished." Here she paused, hardly knowing how Jean would receive this proposition; but the youthful widow had a strength of mind and purpose hardly to be expected from the extreme gentleness of her character and demeanour.

"You are right Bessy," she immediately answered, "I have been expecting this these many days, but dreaded to mention it first. I know you are right; you have been my teacher and protector, Bessy, ever since I was an infant like that (pointing to the cradle); and in my distress you have been like a guardian angel. You have worked in my sickness and helplessness, for my comfort and my childrens'; and it would be selfish and wrong in me to wish to keep you longer from your other duties." But here the full sense of her desolation rushing upon her, she gave way once more to a burst of uncontrollable anguish, and the sisters mingled their tears together.

Jean, however, was the first again to speak. "Never mind this; you shall go then, Bessy, to-morrow, if you will. The master (landlord) has sent to tell me, I may take this year's crop from the farm, and our neighbours have promised to help me to labour it; you will come and help me too, when you have done all that is needed at our father's. And as for me being alone"—here she

---

* *Voar*—is either the act of labouring the ground, and sowing the seed, or the season when these operations are performed.

suppressed, with strong effort, her rising emotion,
" Why I have still the children, and God will be
with me."

To be alone, is, to a Shetland peasant, in Jean's
circumstances, above all things to be avoided;
superstition too often bows down the spirit weakened by grief, and thus it came to pass, that
Bessy's affectionate ministrations in her sister's
cottage, had never suffered that sister to be a night
alone, since her sad widowhood, Jean committed
herself to rest that night, with fervent prayers to
the Stay of the widow and the fatherless, that she
might be blessed with fortitude to meet the affecting ordeal before her on the morrow. The sisters
rose almost equally unrefreshed. Bessy busied
herself during the forenoon, in putting every thing
to rights about the little household; and having
hung on the humble dinner, while the sun was as
yet little past the meridian, she took leave of her
cherished sister. We will not say they parted without tears, but each endeavoured to maintain composure for the other's sake. Sweet tie of sisterly
love ! How often has it soothed the saddest moments of our earthly lot ! How has its sympathy
enhanced our joys, and its self-denial ministered to
our comforts ! A fervent " God be with you !"
were Bessy's parting words, and Jean was alone,
except for her infants. To them she turned, and
braced her mind, and took comfort. In maternal
cares the afternoon passed, and twilight drew on;
more than one of Jean's neighbours stepped in to
offer their assistance, or to be with her through

the night, but she only asked one to milk the cow, while she put her little ones to bed, and firmly saying, she would not mind being alone, she lighted her little lamp, and sat down to her spinning-wheel. Can it be wondered at, that a few sad and anxious thoughts at first oppressed the desolate widow? But her habitual devotional feeling soon subdued them, and having had the afternoon luxury of a little tea, she had not heart to make supper for herself only. With her wheel, whose monotonous sound she almost fancied was cheerful companionship, she busied herself, until she thought the hour of rest was at hand, when she rose to look how high the moon was, before she should retire to her couch. She stood a few minutes at the door, her eyes fixed on the unclouded brilliancy of the lovely planet, when she heard voices and footsteps approaching from the hill-side. Her cottage was separated from the rough trodden pathway, by a low grassy dyke, and she presently saw several men pass close by the gate that led to the humble dwelling. Jean heaved a deep sigh, for the thought instantly struck her, that these were seamen returning to gladden some happy home. Two of the men passed on hastily, after a cheerful "goodnight;" the third leaped the slight wicket, and walked swiftly towards the cottage. Jean stood in the doorway, like one entranced, her breathing almost suspended, her heart beating tumultuously; one step she took forwards, so that the moon shone full on her lovely expressive face; and the young man who approached her, became aware of her presence—

" Jean," said he, in a low thrilling voice of rapture.

" My Willy !" exclaimed Jean, as she fell into her husband's arms.

Sacred be the joy of such a moment ! We shall not attempt to describe it; but who will not readily imagine, that Jean was soon soothed into composure by her Willy's voice,—that the father first received into his arms his yet unseen son and namesake,—that he kissed his first-born without awaking him, reserving till the morning, the joy of meeting his blue eyes, and of trying his power of recognition,—that he poured into Jean's sympathizing ear the tale of his perils and his wanderings,—that she again would not pain him by telling what she had suffered, but only assuring him this was the first night she had been left alone,—and that, finally, the grateful pair bent in devout gratitude before the Giver of all things, blessing him for their re-union. It will also be easily imagined, how Jean appeared in the morning without the badge of widowhood,—how her kind-hearted neighbours congratulated and rejoiced with her,— and above all, how Bessy and Jean wept in each other's arms the tears of overflowing joy, though they had repressed those of sorrow at their parting the day before.

Willy and his companions, when nearly exhausted, had been picked up at sea, by an outward bound American vessel, and after much hardship, and the loss of one of their number, they at length succeeded in working their way home.

The two who returned with Willy, and who lived in his immediate neighbourhood, were not so fortunate as he ; one found the mother of his children dead. She had been ill before he last left her, and her anguish at his supposed fate, brought her speedily to the grave. The other young man, by his sudden entrance so alarmed his mother and her neighbours, as to cause serious injury to them. Jean's better regulated mind ensured for her a meeting of unalloyed happiness.

CHAPTER XII.

THE FOWLER.

FOWLING is not pursued in Shetland, as it is in St Kilda and in the Faroe Islands, as a regular branch of employment. On the contrary, the Shetland landlords, and other superiors, by every means discourage their dependants from spending their time and energies in an occupation so desultory and dangerous, and which, moreover, robs the rocks, otherwise so bare and desolate, of those feathered denizens which are their appropriate ornament. Still, so fascinating and exciting is this method of idling away time which might be much more profitably and improvingly employed, that many of the fishermen frequent the cliffs, and peril their lives in the forbidden pursuit. They do not, however, as in most other places where fowling is practised, act in concert, and with the assistance of ropes or rather cables, but contrariwise, steal to the crags as to a prohibited gratification, carefully concealing from their families and neighbours whence comes the evening's feast of wild-fowl eggs, or broiled kittiwakes.

Serious accidents occasionally take place. Some time ago, a man met a very dreadful fate. He had been creeping into a crevice of rock where there were several nests with eggs; having inserted half of his body, he had dislodged a stone, which held him fast. His decaying corpse was found some time afterwards; the head, shoulders, and out-stretched hand, jammed in the crevice, and the feet and legs hanging out.

More lately a man noted for his fowling depre-dations, went out one fine morning, at the early dawn, to gather shell-fish bait for the next day's fishing. It happened to be the day after the Com-munion Sabbath, when there is divine service at noon. The fisherman's Sunday clothes were laid ready, his family went to church, and returned, but he appeared not. Night came, and he was yet absent. Still his family were under no particular anxiety, imagining he had gone to a relation's house at some little distance. In the morning, however, when he did not join his boat's crew for the usual fishing, the alarm was given, and inquiry and search were immediately instituted. Inquiry and search, however, proved unsuccessful for a considerable time, but finally, near the brink of a precipice, where a cleft in the rock made an accessible way for a short distance downwards, the poor man's shoes and basket of bait were found. Nothing more could be seen from above; but his fishing associates proceeded in their boat to the base of the cliff, from which they thought they perceived some-thing like a human form. With renewed hope they climbed up, and found their unfortunate comrade caught between two rocks, where he was easily re-

clining, as if asleep; but he had fallen from a great
height, and was quite dead. And by this act, as
of a truant schoolboy, for a few wild-fowl eggs, a
wife and large family were left destitute and
mourning.

There is in the island of Unst, one man, who,
by his bravery, expertness, and, we may perhaps
add, his incorrigible perseverance, has gained a
tacit immunity from the general restriction; his
poaching misdemeanours, as they may be called,
being at least winked at.

His father had also been a noted fowler, and
since his own earliest boyhood, he has made it his
pastime to scramble amongst the steepest crags
and cliffs, making many a hair-breadth escape—
many an unheard of prize. He has plundered the
most inaccessible nooks, and even surprised the
eagle in her nest. He climbs barefooted, and his
toes clasp the slippery rock as talons would. Fear
or dizziness he knows not, and for a few shillings
or for an afternoon's recreation, he will scale many
a high and rugged precipice, and penetrate many
a time-worn crevice, where human foot but his
own will probably never tread. Every cranny,
every stepping place in the most precipitous headlands of his native island is intimately known to
him, and at what expense of indomitable perseverance, adventurous explorings, and undaunted
courage this has been accomplished we may not
stop particularly to relate.

On one occasion, led on by his unconquerable
desire of adventure, he had passed almost unwit-

tingly to a point of an overhanging cliff, to which even he, or his oracle—his father, had never before dared to venture. His object was to discover the spot where he believed a pair of eagles had long built unmolested. Overjoyed he reached the place, and triumphantly possessed himself of the eggs, (for which by-the-by a commercial collector afterwards paid him *five shillings!* a mean imposition, as they were worth thirty or forty.) Then, for the first time, our adventurer became aware of his whereabouts. He paused a few moments, not in fear, but in unfeigned surprise, how he could have got there; and then the consideration arose, how should he return? It ought to be mentioned for the benefit of the un-initiated, that it is always much more difficult to get down, than to ascend. The whole tortuosities and difficulties of the path are less distinctly in view; hence the adventurer cannot so readily and safely choose his footing, and, besides, when looking down from a great height, the head is never so steady. In the present case, moreover, the object was attained—the excitement was past, and it is well known, how wonderfully the blood cools, and the courage becomes calculating, in these latter circumstances.

Well—beside the plundered eyrie, our gallant fowler sat cogitating,—"I'll never return—to begin with—that's certain," he said aloud to himself, "after all my escapes and exploits my time is come at last,—well, if it is so, it is,—let me meet my fate like a man. If it is not come, I shall get down safely, as I have done before, though never

from such an awful place as this!" He then, as
he says, precipitately began the descent, plunging
on with no defined ideas, except his early imbibed
belief in predestination, and an occasional aspiration to the Almighty for protection. He never
knew how or by what route he reached a place of
comparative safety, but he would not " attempt
that spot again for twenty guineas !"

It is not, however, only in those localities with
which from childhood he has been familiar, that
our fowler is dexterous and adventurous in his
undertakings. Tempted by an offer of adequate
reward, from an amateur, he engaged to procure
an eagle's egg from a distant quarter, as the Unst
eyrie had been already robbed that season. In
the few days interval of his absence the gentleman was extremely uneasy—greatly repenting that
he had offered the bribe, though he had by no
means urged the step. But in due time the brave
cragsman returned successful, having *twice* scaled
the precipice to near the nest. The first time,
when he reached the place whence he scared the
parent birds, he found their nestling place so
situated, under an overhanging rock, that though
he saw the eggs, he could not by possibility reach
them. Nothing daunted, he returned, and made his
preparations. To the end of a long fishing-rod, he
attached a bladder, the mouth of which he kept
distended by a wire ; reaching this simple, but in-
genious apparatus from the nearest perching place,
where he leaned, he succeeded in gently edging the
eggs into the bladder, and so bore them off in

triumph. It was the most lucrative, though one of the most dangerous adventures he had ever accomplished, for the place was strange to him,—the weather was stormy,—and the birds were so fierce, as to be often in startling proximity to the spoiler.

But the crowning feat of this man's daring was, his surprizing a sea-eagle in her own nest, and capturing her. The same thing, indeed, had been done by his father fifty years ago, but we are ignorant if any person elsewhere ever accomplished such an achievement.

Our adventurer had been aware for several years, that the eagles, whose eyrie he sometimes robbed, had found a still higher and more concealed place for their nestling. Long he searched for the spot, and patiently he cowered and watched, until one day he saw the parents engaged in building their nest, but it seemed to him a place inaccessible, even to his skill. Enthusiastic as the man is, he nevertheless adopts every prudent precaution for safety; and it is not always that the state of the rocks,—the weather,—and his own feelings will permit him to make such a bold attempt as that which he now meditated. At length he could refrain no longer, and on a calm day in the spring, after he had made the local discovery, with a clear head, and steady foot, he attained the wished for elevation. On reaching the immediate neighbourhood of the spot, he saw the white tail of the parent bird, as brooding on her eggs, it projected over the shelf of rock on which she had built her nest. Perceiving that she

K

was not aware of his proximity, owing to the noise-lessness of his approach, and an intervening projection of rock, the dauntless man flung himself with outspread arms on the back of the powerful and ferocious bird. She seemed to be completely cowed by the suddenness and vigour of the assault, for she made no resistance.

In what a situation did the fowler now find himself? We can scarcely imagine one more terrible—perhaps we might say sublime! He was on a flat ledge of rock, a few feet square,—an over-hanging precipice an hundred feet above him,—while underneath, at six times that distance, roared the ocean abyss,—and screaming around him, soared the male eagle, as if hesitating whether or not to attack the spoiler of his home. His coolness and self-possession, however, carried him through triumphantly. First he twisted together the strong wings of his captive,—then loosening his garters, with one he bound her bill, and with the other her legs. Thus fettered and gagged she lay at his mercy, and he paused a few minutes to take breath, and ask himself what now he should best do. He greatly wished to preserve his captive uninjured, as a questionless voucher for the extraordinary tale he would have to tell, but loaded thus, he felt he could not attempt the dizzy path by which he must return; so, after a few anxious cogitations, he threw his prize over the precipice! Bound and helpless, she dashed from rock to rock as she fell, till she rested in a crevice he knew was easily accessible to him from below, and then he commenced his eager and cheery descent, hazardous enough to any one but himself. He soon reached the poor eagle, where she lay struggling with the remains of life, but only slightly mangled, though after a fall so terrific. Her bereaved mate followed the robber on his homeward route, soaring low, and screaming fearfully; but he was never seen again. To his landlord the adventurer at once carried his prize, and having, with extraordinary enthusiasm, told his tale, he received a handsome present, and unqualified praise for the bravery and skill he had displayed. Indeed, even against one's better judgment, it is nearly impossible to refuse approving sympathy with such an exploit.

This man, in every respect, is the *beau-ideal* of an expert fowler. He is but little past the proud prime of life; about medium stature, active, slender, agile, and lithe as an eel, and with an eye that rivals the falcon's in its "piercing ken." He is a good fisherman also; but when other means are scarce, he can materially contribute to the support of a very numerous family, by the produce of such deeds as we have detailed. He has a son, too, the counterpart of himself, who almost as soon as he could walk, was accustomed to climb the rocks with his father, and who is now nearly as dauntless and expert.

With an anecdote or two of "hair-breadth escapes" in the course of Shetland fowling, we shall conclude this sketch.

An enterprizing fisherman, called Eric, a native

of the wildest part of the west side of the country, was understood to be addicted to rambling on the cliffs and precipices; but for the reasons we have previously adverted to, he heedfully concealed the fact. As it was not for gain, and as he dared not speak of his feats, his sole motive in the ventures he made, must have been the love of enterprize and of surmounting difficulties.

On a certain occasion he was won to allow a young gentleman, the son of his pastor, who had somehow wormed himself into his confidence, to accompany him on a hair-brained expedition of this sort; all the more inexcuseable, that the man was twice the age, and ought to have had five times the sense of the youth he was thus teaching to love exploits so needlessly hazardous. They were slowly passing along a narrow path-way, in the face of the precipitous cliff. Above rose the mural rock, three hundred feet beneath was the blue depths of the sea. The slippery shelving which supported them, was barely wide enough for the sole of one foot, so that instead of the usual mode of walking, it was necessary they should slide one foot forward, and then draw the other after it. The lad, not quite a novice in such scenes either, was closely following his companion, when the latter suddenly halted, with—" Dear me ! Maister John, I hae gotten the wrang foot foremost. I'll no get the corner here turned this way."

" What will you do then, Eric?" enquired John—surprised, and a very little flustered.

Eric made no reply; but the youth soon under-

stood how it was ; they had no room to turn themselves, as little could they go backwards ; neither
could the man hope to maintain his balance, if he
tried to get his right foot at liberty so as to take
the dangerous step round the corner at which they
had arrived. He leaned up alongst the rock, took
out his snuff-box, and solaced himself with a hearty
pinch ! He then made a *slight spring in the air*,
changing the position of his feet as he did so. It
was a fearful experiment—a terrific risk ; but it
was bravely made, and safely accomplished. In a
minute more he had placed himself in safety, and
held his hand to his young friend, to assist him
round the point of peril. When their adventure
was fairly over, says John,—

" Eric, were ye no feared man ?"

" An I'd been feared, Maister John, ye and me
had no been here." But he never took " Maister
John" with him again.

In one of the loneliest friths of the North of
Shetland, late on a summer's evening, it is no uncommon thing for any wandering tourist who may
have penetrated there, to see a small boat,—probably the men have had an unsuccessful eela,*—
stealing along the base of a precipice, where sea-
fowls nests are known to be in tempting abundance. The most expert of the boat's crew
ascends the rocks, and quickly catching from
their soft beds the half-fledged gulls and kitti-

* *Eela* is the morning or evening twilight fishing of sillacks
or piltacks.

wakes, throws them over to his companions, who share the booty with him, as the price of their connivance. On one of these occasions a rather ludicrous incident occurred, which, however, too probably might have been a fatal one.

The man who had undertaken to climb the steep bank was neither very experienced nor very brave, though he boasted of being both. He pushed upwards, however, very briskly, without ever looking behind, till he had got to about a hundred and fifty feet, when he stopped to breathe. The pause was fatal to his self-possession, and he called out in tones of horror, " Men—men—I am going—I am going!" He still, however, held on for a little, as it was not till he had shrieked many times, "I am going!" that he did fall headlong. His comrades, having been thus warned, moved the boat out of the way, so that the poor fellow came shear down into the deep water. Mighty was the plunge,—threatening the immersion, but at length he rose to the surface, when of course he was instantly caught hold of, and dragged into the boat. After a good many gasps, and a considerable spluttering of sea water from his mouth, his only remark was, " Eh! men, this is a sad story! I hae lost my snuff-box!"

A young amateur cragsman who often ventured into these forbidden precincts, in search of rare birds and their eggs, for his own or his friends' collections, had so narrow an escape from a fowler's violent death, as for ever cured him of his love for such adventures.

Accompanied by a young lad, he was one day seeking a hawk's nest, and having attained his object, and given his prize to his attendant to carry, he made a little detour for some other trifling object; his own dexterity and former immunity having rendered him perhaps rather careless. The lad was soon seated in safety, looking at his master, who, having scaled the rocks, and dangerous precipice beneath, was mounting on hands and knees the grassy, and comparatively easy slope immediately above them. He had nearly reached the summit, when a piece of stone or turf which he had hold of gave way. In that fearful moment, all the peril before him flashed like lightning on his mind; but he felt also, that calmness, and nothing but calmness, might yet by possibility save him. It was like intuition,—it was more,—it was doubtless the voice of God within, prompting the only means by which his life might be preserved. He rolled for about thirty yards over and over, towards the place where the banks became sheerly perpendicular, and a hundred yards below was a mass of loose rocks, where he must have been dashed to pieces. As he reached the edge of the precipice, and was in the very act of falling, with a powerful effort he swung his body round, and stretched his hands to grasp the ground, which he happily did, and found himself hanging over the abyss, supporting his weight by the strength of his hands and arms only. Had these not been remarkably powerful, and early exercised by gymnastic training, he could not even then have recovered himself; but self-possessed and self-confident,—lifting his heart the while in a momentary supplication for help, he very slowly and cautiously drew himself up, and was soon in comparative safety. Very carefully now he clambered up the slippery, treacherous slope, and, as we have said, never tried fowling again.

CHAPTER XIII.

THE SAILOR.

THE character of seamen is proverbially peculiar and interesting. When the boy, his humble education not merely incomplete, but hardly begun, is set adrift to seek his own livelihood, under the various influences only to be found in sea-faring life, it is no wonder that his tastes and habits receive directions very different from those he would have most probably imbibed on land. Inured to danger, he is brave even to heroism,—unaccustomed to the use or care of money, he is generous even to prodigality.

He is usually frank and truthful, honest and affectionate; on the other hand, he is so habituated to wandering, that he becomes volatile and unstable,—yea inconstant, as the restless element he roams over. His impressions,—and he is very impressible,—are but surface deep, and rarely ever does your thorough bred seaman settle down into a steady home-loving character.

In the Shetland Islands we have numerous opportunities of observing these peculiarities. The men are nearly all of them either fishermen, or seamen in the naval and merchant service. The

former love their homes, cultivate their little fields
in the intervals of their fishing; and should they
escape casualties, live to good old age, surrounded
by children and grand-children. The latter at
first leaving their country for some busy sea-port,
and destitute of even the most common necessaries,
but bearing brave and willing hearts, begin by
making a few summer voyages, and gladden the
home-hearths by spending an occasional winter
there. By-and-by there are longer absences, and
foreign voyages,—letters become more rare, but
money is liberally remitted, and this, in a manner,
compensates for a time for long intervals of fear
and anxiety; then follows "hope deferred," in
many cases total desertion, or uncertain fate; or,
what we cannot help thinking are the least bitter
instances, unprepared-for tidings of sudden death,
spreading sorrow, desolation, and want over the
humble home circle. In such circumstances as
these, the female character often displays much that
is pleasing and praise-worthy,—we would even go
farther, and say, we trust Divine grace implants
and directs what we so often witness of early
widowed maternal love,—its anxious toils and
struggles,—its unwearying self-denial,—its too often
ill-requited sacrifices,—or the meek, uncomplaining
sisterly prayer for the forgetful absent ones,—or
the still deeper hidden shame and disappointment,
and yet forgiveness, of the youthful deserted wife,
or unwedded bride.

Much has been done, and is now doing, for the
long-neglected sailor's best interests,—to strengthen

his good, and correct his wrong propensities, and to lead him in paths of sobriety and God-fearing principle. We hope that those who co-operate actively in this labour of love, will be further strengthened and encouraged, by the reflection, that not with himself alone does the improvement of the poor sailor rest, but that many a lowly home, and many an affectionate breast, is by his well-doing sustained and gladdened.

The following little narrative is designed to illustrate all these remarks. Perhaps it may also suggest or confirm some improving sentiment; at least, it will slightly sketch a few of the manners and customs of a remote and isolated part of our dear fatherland.

Towards the close of a bleak afternoon in the month of April, when the tardy spring in this latitude gives hardly any indication of the approach of a milder season, three persons might have been seen at work in a small field on the borders of one of the voes of Shetland. It was Saturday night, and they worked energetically to complete what remained of the labours of the seed-time. The little party consisted of a handsome young man, and two females; one of the latter was a beautiful girl in her eighteenth year; the other, several years older, but bearing a strong resemblance to her sister, especially in the profusion of golden tresses, and the clear fair complexion, which told they were of the genuine race of ancient Scandinavia. On the elder sister's countenance, which was gentle and pleasing, if not handsome, there

was, on the present occasion, an expression of care
and sadness, while that of the younger beamed
with contentment and joy. Both were clad in
dark blue woollen stuff, of home manufacture, very
suitable for the climate, and very durable, and
therefore thrifty ; but the younger girl wore a becoming cap, tied down with a broad foreign-look-
ing ribbon. There seemed some explanation of
this last attention to personal adornment, in the
demeanour of the young man, who, it might soon
be perceived, was devoted in his attentions to the
maiden by his side. He had been a friendless
orphan child, when the parents of these girls took
him to their home, and brought him up as their
own, and through all the sorrows and privations
of early widowhood, their mother had ever considered him as a son. During their childhood,
Maribel, the elder sister, had been his favourite
and confidant, being nearly of his own age,—and
knowing he was not her brother, he used to say she
should be his wife. Three years, however, before
the evening on which our little narrative commences, the lad, whose name was Magnus, was
seized with the prevailing *mania* for seeing the
world as a sailor. He had returned to Shetland at
the beginning of the previous winter, in shattered
health, to seek in his native breezes and early
home, a solace and shelter from the storms which
had ruthlessly beat on his first voyage in life.

During his absence, Ursula, the lively romping
girl had grown up into the lovely blooming
woman, and to her his heart was soon given, with

all the passionate devotion of manhood's first love. But his health was now restored, and with it his roving propensities returned. He had only remained to assist in finishing the voar, and was therefore now on the eve of departure.

The dull twilight yet lingered, while the young people having accomplished what they were about, and having laid aside their simple primitive tools, took their way to the cottage, the youth's arm round the waist of his beloved, and Maribel following with eyes bent on the ground. The unwonted luxury of tea awaited the family, to celebrate the conclusion of the seed-time; and having partaken of their meal, Ursula began to decorate a cap for church on the morrow, while Magnus watched the progress of the work, and the other females plied their accustomed knitting needles.

During the first pause in the slight conversation, Magnus said, " Well, mother, are my socks and mittens ready, for I must go early in the next week?"

" Stay, dear Magnus, stay with us yet," implored the mother; " we cannot keep the land, except we have some more help to work it."

" You must keep it," returned the young man; " promise me to keep it for two years. I will pay the rent, and two years will soon pass, when I will return and settle, and never leave you more. Promise, Ursula, you will not forget me for two years," and he pressed closer to the side of the girl, whose burning blushes were her only answer; for thus first had he spoken of their at-

tachment, and intended union, before her mother
and grandmother. These exchanged looks of un-
disguised satisfaction at the understood intimation
of Magnus; but at this moment the cottage door
opened, and visitors entered. The foremost was a
good-looking stripling, and he was closely followed
by a man in the early prime of life, above six feet
in height, whose features, though not regular, bore
the impress of sense and good feeling.

Maribel rose hastily, and removed the remainder
of their meal; she would then have stolen away,
had not the young lad prevented her, by playfully
getting between her and the door-way. A short
general conversation ensued, which the younger
visitor led gaily, till jumping up, he exclaimed,
" Good speed to you, Peter, there is no chance for
me I see," glancing at Magnus and Ursula.

" How do you know that?" cried the blushing,
laughing girl. Shaking his head, as if reprovingly
at her, and nodding to the rest, the youth took his
departure. Shortly afterwards the lovers followed,
and the mother recollected that something required attention out of doors, so that her elder
daughter was left with the aged grandmother, and
the remaining visitor, whom they all knew to be a
suitor, though not a favoured one.

During the short embarrassed silence that ensued, Maribel never lifted her eyes from her knitting, but her fingers trembled so violently, that an
initiated eye might have easily detected one loop
after another slipping from the wires, while she
in vain endeavoured to replace them. At length

the old woman spoke. "You are come *from home* to Maribel, Peter?"

"Yes, mother," he replied. "I am just come to ask her from you; and though she has yet given me no encouragement, I hope I shall be more fortunate, if I get your *good word* in my favour."

"You shall have that, right gladly, lad," said the grandmother, whose opinions and authority had justly great weight in her little household; "any girl might be proud of your love, Peter," she proceeded; "and I know of no reason why Maribel should not—My bairn! what is the matter?" she hastily exclaimed, on seeing Maribel burst into a flood of tears.

The young man took her hand, and it trembled wildly. "Why, Maribel," he said, "this distress of yours is not mere maiden shyness. Have I vexed or offended you? I am sure it was far from my meaning to do so."

But still tears in torrents were her only reply. Greatly surprized, her manly lover, on a significant look from the old woman, quitted the cottage, though not the premises, for he lingered in the little yard, and had a consultation with the mother of his beloved, who, however, could only assure him, Maribel had no other more favoured admirer that she knew of.

Meanwhile the poor girl wept in silence, till, on her grandmother pointing out all the advantages of a union with this industrious and respectable young fisherman, and how much joy it would give her aged heart to see her favourite comfortably

settled in life. Maribel replied sadly, " I have no
love for him; I can never be his wife. Tell him
not again to ask me," she added imploringly.

Human nature, it is often remarked, is the same
every where; and in the Shetland cottage, as in
the grandee's palace, worldly advantages are too
often weighed against woman's priceless unbought
affections. Therefore, thus again urged the grandmother. " But tell me, jewel, how is this ? Few
girls would refuse Peter. Can it be my bairn
has any love for another we have not suspected."

On this appeal Maribel gave way at length to
long suppressed feeling, bursting afresh into hyste-
rical weeping, till a ray of light broke on her affectionate parent. " Is it possible, Maribel; you—
you love Magnus ? You used to be his favourite."

" Many times he promised he would never wed
another," sobbed the poor girl, and thus were revealed all her early prepossessions and hopes,
cherished in an ingenuous and unsophisticated heart,
till she was doomed to see the object of her girlish
love, transfer and lavish all *his* affections on her sister,
her darling, her only sister. Soothed and encouraged
by her grandmother's good sense and good feeling,
Maribel poured all her sorrows into her sympathizing bosom, and she had hardly done so, when
Peter re-entered.

" Maribel cannot be your wife," said the old
woman. " I am sorry for it, but I cannot at present urge my precious child farther ; neither ought
you I think."

The lover was deeply affected. " Let me hear

it from your own lips," he said, "I have loved you truly and long, and this is a bitter conclusion to my hopes; yet tell me so yourself, my dear girl," and again he took her hand tenderly and respectfully.

"It is very true, Peter," she faltered, "I wish you a much better wife than I could make you,—ask me no more."

"God bless you then, Maribel," he said in a tone of deep feeling, "I will not, however, seek another, while you remain unmarried. God's peace be with you!"

He slowly rose, and turning back on her a gaze, in which regret and disappointment were blended with ardent affection, he left the little dwelling.

Next evening Ursula wandered on the sea-beach with her lover.

"Go I must, dear girl," he said, as he pressed closer the hand which was clasped in his; "but cheer up, it is only for a time."

"You will never return, Magnus," sighed the maid.

"How can you wrong me by such a suspicion, Ursula?" replied he. "My hopes, my heart, my gratitude, are all centred here; and if my life be spared"—We need not repeat the vows of constancy, which were there mutually pledged. In a day or two Magnus took his final farewell.

Not many months afterwards, the young stripling who had accompanied Peter, as is the custom in Shetland, on his love visit above related, and whom we shall call Charlie, renewed his attentions to the young deserted maiden, who received them,

L

her sister thought, with too much encouragement
for one betrothed to another, and Maribel consequently remonstrated on the subject with the somewhat thoughtless girl.

" I fear, Ursula, you do not love Magnus quite
so well as he does you ?"

" What makes you think so," said the younger ;
" but, indeed, I begin to think he cares little about
me ; he has written but once."

" His situation may not admit of more. Indeed,
indeed, Ursula, you are trifling with his happiness,
and with your own."

" You are so earnest on Magny's behalf," returned Ursula, " perhaps you love him best yourself."

This was said quite at random ; but such an
expression of anguish spread over Maribel's face,
and settled in her meek eye, as at once arrested
the attention of the giddy but affectionate girl, and
revealed her sister's secret.

There are occasions in this world of sorrows,
when the misery of a life seems almost to be con-
centrated in the whirlwind passion of a few
minutes ; and such was the short interval that
elapsed, while either sister gazed into the other's
face, and neither spoke.

At length Ursula murmured,—" Sister, dear,
why did I not know of this before, and I would
not have promised to be his ?"

" Too truly do these words confirm me in my
idea, that you do not love him as he deserves,"
sighed the elder sister.

" I will never marry him, no, never," cried Ursula, with energy, " and you, Maribel, shall."
Maribel only shook her head.

" Do you remember that day so long ago, Maribel, when we were all on the shore gathering shell-fish, and the rapidly flowing tide, before we were aware of it, surrounded the rock on which Magnus was ?"

" Can I ever forget it ?" Maribel breathed in the lowest tones, and with a convulsive shudder.

" You rushed to his help, though the water reached to your waist, while he, helpless and panic-stricken, would not leave his dangerous post without your hand. A few, a very few minutes more, and the rushing sea would have swept him away ; and even as it was, you had almost perished with him. You saved his life that day, Maribel dear, while I could only scream and fly from you both. A sound sleep completely restored poor Magny, but you lay in a fever for days, brought on by the fright and the wetting you had got. You bought his safety dearly, and his you ought to be !"

" Well then," now rejoined Maribel, for she felt it best to be quite candid for the sake of both. " Oft-times, as he ran to my bed-side, he whispered his thanks and fondness, and promised he should never wed another ; we were then under twelve years old, but his childish words were somehow very sweet to me,—often repeated as they were, for years afterwards. Now do I deeply reproach myself for suffering such thoughts to become so entwined with my ideas of earthly happiness, that it seems to me as if all I valued were lying a hapless wreck on the stream of my life. May God lead me to himself, as the rock of my strength, and may he forgive me, that I have been so sorely tempted of late, as to wish sometimes one or both of us had not survived that day I so long regarded as the most fortunate of my life!"

Hitherto poor Maribel appears but as a love-lorn maiden, shrinking from the blast of unrequited affection, but Ursula renewed her offer to resign Magnus for her sister's sake, and knew not till that moment how dear he was to her.

"But he," re-iterated Maribel, "let us think not of ourselves, but of him. He loves you best, Ursula, and Heaven knows his happiness is dearer to me than my own!"

Still Ursula urged her proposition to encourage and marry young Charlie before Magnus should return; and though at first he might be vexed, she said, he would doubtless feel soon, that justice demanded his return to his first allegiance. This Maribel would not for a moment listen to. "We must *do our duty*, sister," she said, "else how can we expect a blessing on our life. You must be faithful, Ursula, to the promise you have given; but your generous feeling to me has at length showed me what I ought to do. I cannot blame Magny, poor fellow, our early orphaned playmate, our kind confiding brother!" and her tears fell fast, but composedly. "He has been swayed by circumstances. On me alone be the sacrifice. I shall feel, in the approval of my own mind, and the blessing of God, a comfort and reward for all it may cost me."

She paused a few moments, and inwardly breathed a prayer for direction and fortitude from on high. "It will so please my mother and grandmother," she proceeded: "Yes, it shall be so!" And this uneducated cottage maiden felt at that moment all the sweetness resulting to a noble mind, from the exercise of self-denial, to promote the happiness of those it loves.

A few weeks sped past, Maribel braced her energies for the course she had resolved on, and the season devoted to rest and festivity in Shetland arrived. Then she no longer turned sedulously from the regards of her still faithful admirer, Peter. A hint from Ursula brought him again to their cottage fireside; and ere spring labour once more commenced, Maribel was his wife,—a step she never had reason to regret; since, in her husband's indulgent tenderness, and the maternal duties that ere long devolved on her, she lost the keen sense of her early disappointment.

It seemed now that Ursula clung to her absent lover with redoubled affection. She discarded all her danglers, and emulating her sister's example, reserved the purest energies of her warm heart, to welcome back the wanderer.

Her constancy was ill requited. The stipulated two years, and many more flew by, and Magnus *never returned* to the cot that had sheltered his homeless childhood, and the hearts that yearned for him there. Once or twice only he wrote; but whether he yet wandered over the world, or slept in a foreign land, or had found a watery grave, his Shetland friends could not learn. They had some reason to believe he was alive, but had forgotten the claims of fatherland, gratitude, and love.

It was not till several years had elapsed, during which she had heard nothing of Magnus, that Ursula was united to a steady young fisherman. She too became a happy wife. Her husband rented the little farm where her fathers had dwelt, and her grandmother and mother still remained with her. But yet amidst the cares of both sisters, a pitying pang often crossed their breast, as memory recalled the loved, but unstable companion of their childhood. Especially at the still hour of the evening prayer, when the *absent* were referred to at the throne of grace, the sighs that slowly breathed from the female lips at that humble fireside, were all for the unforgotten Magnus!

We have said this little family circle had some reason to believe their truant sailor yet lived. A seaman, who, though not a near neighbour, was well acquainted with Magnus in his own island, wrote to his family that he had seen the young man in a foreign sea-port, but strange to say, he denied all recognition ; he bore another name, but that is common with sailors, yet the Shetlandman was certain he was not mistaken,—and indeed he was not.

Years more flitted away, and a stately merchant vessel from New York sailed up the Clyde. Arrived at Greenock, one of the active Christian

agents of the " Bethel Flag Union" visited the
ship, and induced some of the sailors who manned
her, to attend divine worship in the evening.
Among these, was one who had been for ten years
an exile,—who had been in peril and in wreck,—
in sickness, and also in much sin and forgetfulness
of the God who had so often preserved him. He
was, though weather-beaten, a fine looking man,
but his eyes were not lifted proudly or fearlessly,
they rather sought the ground, and avoided the
gaze of others. Perhaps this might be humility ;
yet to one who observed him, it seemed shame.
Was it shame to find himself there ?—or was it
shame that he had been so long absent from divine
service ? Probably there might be a mingling of
both feelings.

Again and again he attended the simple, solemn
worship, under the blessed Bethel flag, and at
length he was addressed by his long unheard *home
name.*

The natural start and ingenuous glow over the
swarthy cheek,—the glistening enquiring eye,—
and then the subdued answer, in which was detected by the questioner, the peculiar and rarely
conquered Shetland accent and tone,—all told a
countryman that Magnus would not now disown his
fatherland and friends.

He afterwards avowed, as many others have
done, that it was the thrilling melody of a psalm
tune, once loved, and never heard since he left his
island home, that melted the stout and careless

heart which had withstood many a louder *spoken* warning, and that led him back to the spot where he might hear it again, and this paved the way for a meek reception of the Gospel truths there so faithfully and affectionately set forth. The wanderer was reclaimed,—the prodigal thought of his father's house at last.

A letter,—a long penitential letter, couched in sincere, and even eloquent language, and pleading for pardon, very soon consoled the motherly and sisterly hearts. Magnus had been informed that both the latter were married, and Ursula's husband instantly answered the letter in the name of all.

Then were sent a golden sovereign, and several more valuable and acceptable presents, with a promise of a visit ere long, and an assurance, *with God's help*, of unchanging dutifulness for the future.

The winter just before the last, was a peculiarly stormy one, and the Shetland Islands were strewn with wrecks. One morning, after a fearful gale, the adopted mother of Magnus, now stooping under the weight of years, and recent unavoidable hardships, had crept down to the sea-beach near her dwelling. A poor dog, dripping and half-drowned, struggled through the subsiding surf to the woman's feet. It had been a fine and powerful animal, but was now quite exhausted, so that though the family endeavoured to warm and revive it, it gave a few gasps, and expired. The dog had round its neck a

leathern collar, with a brass-plate, and what were
the feelings of these Shetlanders, when they read,
engraved on that plate, the name of the ship, her
master, and the town to which she belonged,—
the very ship in which their recently recovered
Magnus had written he was to sail for Newfoundland on a short voyage. It was indeed a short
one,—and it was his last poor fellow.

Mysterious was that Providence which snatched
the reclaimed prodigal to Himself, ere his newly
formed resolutions were too severely tried, and
which led his vessel, by adverse gales, to perish so
near the humble but peaceful home, he had so long
and waywardly despised. It was with shivering
terror and suspense, the beach was searched for
days after the dog came on shore, lest perchance
some bodies might be found there; but there was
nothing seen, save a few of the smallest fragments
of a wreck, disclosing painfully how total had been
the destruction of the vessel from which the poor
dog had escaped for the time.

From a deep feeling of sympathy and interest
in the affecting incident last mentioned, some
pains were taken to ascertain if the conversion to
God, of the poor sailor, was real and decided, and
so far as could be learned, the inferences are most
favourable.

His last act, before leaving port, was to settle it
so, that a small sum which would be due at his
death, should be paid to his adopted mother;
and this, with the carefully preserved sovereign,
and the dog's collar, is all that remains of this

Shetland sailor, to his attached and sorrowing
friends.   May the blessing of the Most High speed
the friends of the " Bethel Flag," without whose
kind offices they would not have had even these,—
the sad but dear memorials of the loved and lost.

CHAPTER XIV.

THE KNITTERS.

FISH being the most valuable commodity of the
Shetland Islands, and its produce and pre-
paration for the market being the chief ostensible
dependance of the people, the cares of the house,
and labour on the little farms, are left in a great
measure to the females. Only in seed-time and
harvest, do the men, as a general rule, give anything like steady assistance in the working of the
land. The industry of the men then is but desultory. Because of the uncertainty of the weather,
they will remain many days at their lodges, waiting, and doing nothing while they wait, for the
favourable moment to put off to sea. It were
greatly to be desired, that they would employ these
unfilled-up hours, with some light and handy occupation,—knitting for example, which appears to be
every way suitable ; but unfortunately they consider it so scornfully effeminate, that we have heard
of only one or two men who are good knitters;
and they are ashamed to avow it, and practise it
only in secret; and yet the Highland, Irish, and
Faroe men, make considerable sums by the knitting of coarse hose and seamen's frocks.

The Shetland females, on the other hand, are constantly and energetically industrious,—not only in hoeing potatoes, making hay, and drying and grinding corn, but in such heavy work, as carrying sea-weed for manure,—digging the ground with the spade, and harrowing in the seed. And then, every moment that is not occupied in these and other necessary operations of the household and farm, is filled up with knitting. You will never see a Shetland woman without work of this kind in her hand,—whether with her keyshie of peats on her back, or seated on the sober pony, with which she goes often several miles to bring home dried moor-grass for fodder, or fish from the sea-side,—whether talking to you, or paying or receiving a visit,—all the while she plies swiftly the knitting-pins or wires. The younger women, whose sight is still good, and whose fingers are supple, have always two pieces of worsted work in progress at a time,—the brown wool stocking for odd moments, or in the twilight, or when going about,—and the fine lace-like shawl or veil, for the long evenings, or half holiday in which the daughters of a family indulge themselves in turn. Socks for home use, or for sale, are always the work of the old women.

There being no sort of manufactories, or openings for the regular industry of the females, excepting only knitting, they have happily so applied themselves to this art, as to have brought it to great perfection, and secured for it a pretty regular demand, to which also the peculiar softness and

fineness of the native wool, no doubt in a considerable measure contributes.

The sheep of Shetland are of a peculiar breed,
indigenous to the country. They are very small,
and, of course, wild and hardy. Strangers, indeed,
who see these little, odd-looking creatures, shy as
deer, scampering along at a speed almost as great,
can hardly be persuaded they are of the sheep
genus at all.

The liberty of pasturage on the uninclosed commons, is included in the holding of the fisherman's
small farm. The people, therefore, keep as many
animals as they can, and the pastures consequently
are always overstocked.

Most of the cottars have a few sheep, and some
more fortunate or more careful than their neighbours, have stocks of from twenty to a hundred,
which are all marked in a peculiar manner in the
ears, each family retaining through generations its
own mark. They are never folded or fed, but at
certain intervals, are driven by dogs, and a multitude of owners, to small ponds (or *croos*), for the
purpose of being counted, marked, rooed, or occasionally taken for sale or slaughter. Comparatively few are doomed to the fate last mentioned, as the animals are chiefly valued for their
wool; but severe seasons, and other casualties, to
which the more than half-wild creatures are subject, prevent them from increasing, as they might
do, under a better regulated system. The ewes
hardly ever have more than one lamb at a birth,
and, in consequence of sufficient males not being

reserved, the females often do not bring forth at all. Moreover, worrying dogs and sheep-stealing *bipeds* commit great depredations on the flocks with absolute impunity. It might, one should think, be easily so managed by the proprietors of the soil, that no tenant should have above a stipulated number of sheep on the common,—that a proper proportion of rams should be retained,—and that some local supervision should be appointed for the prevention of *robbery* and *murder*. The cottagers being for the most part tenants at will, the landlords possess great power over them, which in days gone by, they have been accused of discreditably abusing. It would seem, they have *now* run to the opposite extreme of indulgence, and too much neglect to exercise, in a wholesome enlightened manner, the influence which their situation gives them. Passing strange indeed it appears that most of the Shetland lairds are so blind to their own interest, in which, of course, that of their dependents are involved, as to neglect all regulation and oversight in the breeding both of sheep and of ponies. On the former, a large proportion of the people's resources depends; and the latter, now almost equally disregarded, might be made even more productive of valuable returns.

The Shetland sheep are of various colours, besides black and white. They are of almost every shade of brown and grey, and some are piebald. The wool is also of very different quality, even on the same animal, the finest being about the throat and back. Nevertheless, even the coarser portions

have a velvety softness, quite peculiar. Several
causes have been assigned for this distinguishing
property, besides the exclusiveness of the breed.
One is the scant but often highly aromatic pasture of the Shetland hills, and another, that the
wool is never shorn, but *rooed*, that is, pulled with
the fingers from the creature's back, lock by lock.
It must be remembered, that sheep, like many
other animals, yearly change their coating. Hence,
as the season advances the wool becomes loose; the
animal then rubs it along the heather, which acts
as a comb; and, indeed, a fair wool harvest is often
gained in this way by the poorer ownerless persons,
who gather what is left among the stones and
heath. At the time then, when the fleece bcomes
loose, which is in June, about a month after lamb-
ing time, the sheep are collected, and their wool
plucked off by women, who are sufficiently tender
in the operation, so that the rooing gives no pain,
but is rather relief to the animal. There is, moreover, left on the skin, a considerable quantity of
long hair, provided by nature for several species of
animals in northren latitudes to protect them more
completely from the inclemency of the weather, and
this, it is obvious, would be totally removed were
shears employed on the sheep.

The wool being brought home, is carefully separated into its different colours and qualities. There
is nothing of which the Shetland housewife is so
proud, or takes so much care, as her stock of
wool. The coarsest is set aside for the fisherman's
socks and mittens; a second quality is used for a

sort of twilled blanketing, woven by some super-
annuated fishermen, in a very primitive handloom.
This *claith* (so it is called), if grey or mixed, is dyed
with indigo, and makes very durable jackets and
trousers ; if white, it is used for blankets and pet-
ticoats, or under-shirts for the men. The brown
wool is almost entirely made into ladies' stockings,
and the best of the grey into gentlemen's socks, of
which a few pairs will always be found, on inquiry, in
every cottage, awaiting an opportunity of sale. If
none else offers, these hose are bartered at the
shops for cotton goods, or any other sort of clothing the seller may require ; and, in general, it is
understood, in this system of exchange, that the
merchants require considerable profits to secure
themselves against risks, and to allow for freights,
&c. A greater loss arises to the poor cottars, from
travelling pedlars, who tempt them with worthless
trumpery, and carry off the produce of their industry at very low prices.

The spinning is all done by hand on a common
lint-wheel. The staple of the wool is very short,
and it is said, cannot, on that account, be so well
managed by machinery. The same circumstance
accounts also for the fact, that Shetland hose, however pleasant in wear, are not very durable.

The finest wool is not carded, but combed out,
and then teased by the fingers. It is mixed with
grease, or a little fine oil, and a few persons who
are very expert can spin, from two ounces of raw
wool, *six thousand yards* of three-ply thread,—a sufficient quantity to make a good sized shawl. This

process is very tedious, and requires manipulation so nice, that very few persons ever attain the art in perfection. More usually a veil may be made of half an ounce, and a shawl of four or five ounces of wool. This will serve to explain, that unlike Berlin and other wools, which are sold by weight, and spun by machinery, the finer the thread of Shetland worsted, the more the labour; it is therefore disposed of by the cut or number of threads.

Shetland has been celebrated for beautifully fine plain knitting, for the last century at least, and produced gloves for ten shillings and sixpence, and stockings for two guineas a pair, knitted on wires as fine as a sewing needle.

It is believed the Duke of Medina Sidonea, admiral of the Spanish Armada, and his followers, whose ship was wrecked on Fair Isle, and who afterwards wintered in Shetland, were the first that taught these islanders the art of knitting. Certain it is, that the painted-like manufacture of the Fair Isle people at this day, is quite similar to what is made in the South of Spain. But the open work knitting now so attractive to the poor artists, as well as to the public, is an invention for which the Shetland females themselves deserve all the credit. From the simplest beginnings, led on and encouraged by some ladies as a pastime, it has progressed from one thing to another, till it has attained its present celebrity, without the aid either of pattern-book, or of other instruction, than the diligence and taste of the natives themselves.

We are, indeed, aware, that in Madeira, Germany, Malta, &c., very fine specimens of knitting in cotton and silk threads are produced; but after making every possible enquiry, we cannot make out, that they were in advance of the Shetlanders in the invention of the art; still less, that the latter, since the days of the shipwrecked admiral aforesaid, have ever received any foreign instruction whatever in knitting. In confirmation of this statement, should such be required, we may just mention, that the patterns and terms here used in knitting, have a nomenclature all their own. A Shetland knitter cannot comprehend a pattern from a book, if one is shewn to her; and should you attempt a translation for her benefit, she will hardly have patience to follow it,—ten times more quickly than you can read it, move her fingers and her thread, and ere the design is half completed, she knows what is intended, and finishes,—probably improves upon it, without more assistance.

In seasons of ordinary mildness, when the men may get pretty regularly to sea, and the corn is not shaken by September gales ere it is ripe, and the potatoes do not fail, the Shetland cottars are, with common care, tolerably comfortable. They must work rather hard, it is true, yet certainly not harder than labourers elsewhere; and they have the advantage of being removed from many fluctuations in trade and manufactures, which often tell so hard on the labouring classes in otherwise more favoured latitudes. They are, if the expression may be allowed, more completely in the hands of Providence, since soft favouring weather is nearly all they require for a state of prosperity. But the ordinary course of events shews, that this is not to be expected in the geographical position of the country. Summer mildew, and harvest gales, often damage the crops, while frequent squalls, or heavy seas, render the fishing season unproductive or disastrous. Under these circumstances the knitting is a resource, the importance of which may hardly on a cursory view be estimated; and we trust the British public will not soon lose their taste for the handiwork of the poor Shetland artists.

Numerous instances might be adduced of whole families being rescued from absolute want, and even the rent of many a widowed mother paid, by the industry of the females in knitting alone, especially since the introduction of the fancy articles, where there is so much room for taste and application.

By the last census, the whole population in Shetland was deficient nearly a third in males. This arises in a great measure from the absence of the sailor part of the families, which, with the circumstance, that so many casualties befal the men at home, renders it quite common for whole households to be composed of only women and children. It may, indeed, be satisfactorily calculated, that three-fourths of the income of the Islands, if Lerwick be excluded, is assignable to the agency of the female sex. Let us sketch one little picture of Shetland life, that may perhaps illustrate some of these remarks.

One fine autumnal day, two strangers were returning from a pedestrian excursion to the western coast. Their feet were soaked with wet; their hands begrimed; their guns shouldered, and a fine water-spaniel trotted wearily at their heels. Thinking to make a short cut to their destined lodging for the night, they leaped a low fence of rough stones, topped with crumbling turf, and were crossing the little paddock it inclosed, when they perceived two females, seated on the grass, beside a small stack of peats, belonging to a cottage so low, it had been concealed from the strangers by a slight inequality of the ground. As they drew near, two girls rose respectfully to their feet, and the travellers stopped to ask their way. One of the girls seemed a little above twenty, of middle size, and gentle expression of countenance, and she was clad in tolerably tidy and deep mourning. The other was taller, but much more girlish in figure. Her dress consisted of a blue woollen petticoat, and a dark coloured jacket of cotton, over which was a 'kerchief of rusty black, and a broad band of the same sable hue tied down a coarse muslin cap. In her hand she held a half-finished sock she was knitting, over which she bent, turning at the same time half away, to conceal her face, for she was, and had been, weeping bitterly.

Of the strangers, we need only say, that one was young, heavily laden with multifarious trophies of his ramble, and looked like a student. His companion, who was the spokesman, was of middle size, and noble presence. Grounding their fowling-

pieces, the travellers seated themselves on the turf-
dyke, and the dog also gladly stretched himself for
a rest, while a short colloquy took place. The
lonely dwelling of which the girls seemed to be the
inmates, was built on the common, a usual practice
for the helpless females, who are not able to pay a
farm rent; because, if their friends will only raise
for them the little cottage, they have nothing
to pay for permission to occupy the site, and
perchance inclose and break up a few roods of
the thin barren soil, in which to plant some potatoes, with their peat ashes for manure. Annie,
the elder sister, explained this to the stranger,
who further asked of their parentage and employments; and, by the kindliness of his eye, and the
sympathy of his words and manner, he soon learnt
their simple history. Their father had been lost
at the haff, long, long ago,—they did not remember
him,—their mother had died a few days before ;—
and both the girls wept again. They had a
brother, he was far away at sea, they knew not
where,—grief and anxiety respecting him had
shortened their mother's life, and saddened her last
hours. In the low hut,—the home of that mother's
widowhood, there lived also an unmarried aunt,
who attended to every thing; they loved her well,
and she cherished them as her own. They had,
moreover, a bed-ridden grandmother, who had a
small pension from a merchant-seaman's fund, to
which her deceased husband had subscribed, and
this pittance of about two pounds a-year, was all
the worldly dependance of this poor family, ex-

cepting what they earned by knitting It was a
most beautiful shawl that Annie held in her hands,
nearly finished. "Aunty Mabel" knitted socks;
she could do a pair in a week, except when she was
spinning; their father's brother, who had a large
family of his own, had given them a pet-lamb, which
was now a " fine wooled" ewe, so that they had a
little wool from her and her yearly lamb; sometimes
they bought a little, and sometimes they worked
in their neighbours' fields a few days for some
more. Annie had been able, by the sale of some
work, to purchase for herself decent mourning for
her dear mother; but Britta, the younger sister,
had lately lived with her uncle, where she had to
work so constantly on the farm, and in the dairy,
she had no leisure for knitting; she had not even
learnt the open work patterns; and she was now
crying because " she could not go to the kirk, or
any where, without right claes."

It may be observed here, that the Shetland
peasants, both men and women, but especially the
latter, never go abroad unless they are respectably
clad. They have a decent pride in this, which is
very creditable to them. Strangers often remark it,
and because they witness not rags and squalor, are
led to think the people are in better circumstances
than is consistent with fact. But they do not see
the shivering children, and crouching old people,—
many of the latter kept *to bed* for lack of raiment; or
the borrowing from one another, even of those who
are at church, and otherwise seen abroad; or the
shame with which many a hard-working wife will

hide herself, even from her neighbours, that her girls may have the use of her best things. But to return to Annie and the kind looking stranger.

" Does not the uncle with whom she stays give your sister clothing as well as food ?" asked he.

" Oh no," replied Annie, " even his own wife and daughters supply themselves with clothes by their handiwork. It's all the custom here, sir."

" And why not *thus* your sister also ?" demanded the gentleman.

She was silent. It was too evident the cousins took the time for their own knitting they denied to poor orphaned Britta.

" And when or how is this probation to end ?" pursued the stranger.

A slight respectful gesture shewed the cottage maiden did not understand the query.

" When does your sister expect she may procure what she wants ?" explained he.

" Oh ! she will get a har'st fee in a while," Annie answered.

" She must then wait till after harvest !—Is that shawl you are making for sale ?"

" No, Sir. I got the yarn from a lady to knit it for her."

" But you will be paid for your work."

" Oh, yes, sir ! but I owe something at the shop for my shoes. Aunty Mabel needs greatly some tea, and we have the casting of our peats to pay for yet."

" You would help your sister if you could, would you not ?"

"Oh! blithely that sir," said Annie, while a more winning softness stole into her eye, "I have just been telling her that before har'st is come yet, I will have two or three veils made, and I will give her them to buy a black frock with."

"By-the-by," abruptly said the younger traveller, "have you a draught of milk you could let me have?"

"We have no milk," responded Annie, "but some good *blaand ;* shall I get you some?"

"*Blaand !* what may that be?"

"The whey of churned milk sir," smiled Annie, "it is the only drink we have, but it is very good, we get as much as we like from our neighbours who have *kye.*"

"Blaand by all means then," said the strangers together, and Britta instantly stepped to the cottage, soon returning with a small bowl of whey.

It proved sharply acidulous, and very refreshing to the weary and thirsty pedestrians.

"And now, have you not a pair or two of socks you could let me have," continued the elder stranger.

"Aunty has," promptly replied Annie, "But I fear only one pair finished; and again Britta was despatched to bring them.

The travellers then saw her face looking somewhat brighter. It was not beautiful, but the red pouting lips, and the long thick lashes shading soft eyes of bluish grey, made it look very sweet and interesting. The mass of crisply curling hair, was intended to stay under the close mourning cap, but one side during her weeping had fallen over her cheek dishevelled in wavy ringlets many a high-bred beauty would have envied. Hastily pushing back the stray locks, and having dried her tears, she looked so charming that both the travellers gazed at her admiringly, while she presented the soft wool socks to the benevolent looking gentleman. Pulling out his purse, he put a piece of money into her hand, and the strangers went their way.

They had scarcely proceeded twenty yards when Britta exclaimed, " Annie ! it's gold, it's not a *shilling!*" " Run after them, Britta," cried her sister. But Britta hung back from bashfulness and dread of strangers, whom she had hardly ever in her life before spoken to. Annie therefore hurried after the pedestrians, carrying the sovereign, and explained the mistake.

" Dear me !" exclaimed their kindly looking friend. " A sovereign !—so it is,—never mind, I cannot possibly take it back. Let your sister buy her mourning dress. Providence sent it her for that purpose, I suppose."

Annie was so surprised, she often afterwards thought, how strange it was, she had not even thanked the giver.

But needs it be told how Britta was cheered,—what a nice cup of tea, " granny" and " aunty" had that evening,—how Britta appeared at the kirk next Sunday,—and how, with more shrewdness than her gentler sister, she ever believed, the unknown had made no " mistake," but delicately intended the gracious and most acceptable present.

And, moreover, Britta stayed with her sister, instead of toiling hardly through a wet harvest for the fee not now needful. Thus she learnt thoroughly the finest knitting patterns, and very soon their joint work, with aunty Mabel's thrifty management, was sufficient to maintain them all in tolerable comfort, a consummation apparently very far off, had it not been for the stranger's well-timed gift.

CHAPTER XV.

THE WHALE HUNT.

ALTHOUGH a whale hunt has been frequently described as one of the most novel and exciting scenes in Shetland life, yet as any sketches of these Islands would seem incomplete without it, we shall here give it a slight notice.

When we find man enslaving or destroying such creatures as the elephant, the giraffe, and the kingly lion;—still more, when we see him contending in another element, with the gigantic whale, we naturally feel the stirrings of conscious gratification, that animals such as these, fierce and savage to all other species, should be so overawed by comparatively trifling force, when directed by reason, as to crouch, cowed and subdued, and almost at once to yield up their terrific powers to the control of *one*, whom by a single stroke they could destroy. The moral aspect then of the whale-fishing, is as grand in its bearings, as it is satisfying in its results.

We all doubtless remember the exciting scene described in "The Pirate," of a large whale having got embayed in the voe, near Burgh-Westra, which, after sustaining a forenoon's battle, and receiving many wounds, finally escaped to his native depths. About thirty years ago, one of these large whales did actually, in the course of its peregrinations, run itself aground in the shallow of one of the Shetland voes. Being unable to turn, and the tide happening to be on the ebb, it was soon destroyed by many an eager hand. It lay like an island in water four fathoms deep, and a six-oared boat was rowed into its enormous jaws when distended. It was eighty feet long, and its sides could be ascended only by means of ladders from the boats. Many visitors came from distant parts to see this rare spectacle, and more than one *pic-nic* was partaken of on its shoulders.

More lately, another large and valuable whale was found completely jammed, and nearly dead, in a very narrow and lonely geo, where it was despatched with little trouble, by two or three fishermen. They wisely kept the matter a profound secret, and thus obtained a noble windfall, although the animal having been diseased, was not so fat as usual. Any whale of this very large size, as Sir Walter Scott intimates, is one of the Admiralty rights; but of course salvage is allowed to those engaged in its capture and death. It may just be observed, in passing, that the salvage hitherto, has been in all cases of whales and shipwrecks, especially the latter, much too niggard, which has given rise to some abuses. The Crown, in the case of small whales, however, now waives its right of third share, in favour of the captors, a liberality which is most gratefully appreciated.

The " Bottle-nose Whale," *Delphinus Deductor*, is the more usual visitant to our coasts. Hundreds of this species are pretty frequently killed at a time in Shetland, while in Faroe they are reckoned by the thousand every season.

In Shetland the bays are in general not accessible enough from the ocean; or those that are so, do not afford the shelter these animals seem to seek. The people, moreover, are not sufficiently amenable to discipline or law, in respect of the hunt, so that for lack of due concert and regulation, the whales are quite as often frightened off, as driven on shore. The animal in question, we may state, is also called the " Cáaing Whale," from its being easily driven (vernacular, " cáaed"), like a flock of sheep to the slaughter. It is gregarious and migratory in its habits, and roams over the north seas in vast herds, when it is very desirable to Shetlanders and others, that a wing, or light division of the army, should occasionally disobey orders, and lose its way in some exploratory or foraging expedition.

Imagine a calm dull morning, especially after some days of stormy unsettled weather. A child, or perchance a woman, appears at a cottage door, uttering the magic words "whales in Haroldswick," or Gulberwick or Dale's Voe, as the case may be. By the way, some very amusing practical jokes have been perpetrated thus on a neighbourhood of Shetlanders, though public opinion is very properly vehement against such hoaxes. Every man starts as at the bugle call for battle; one throws down the straw he is weaving into ropes or simmonds, and keyshies, and almost sets his dwelling in a blaze by forgetting the hearthstone and sleeping embers are so near—*n'importe*, he leaves the women to look to that. Another tosses aside the awl and leather, with which he is making a pair of shoes— in a great hurry the moment before. A third, an active stripling, upsets his ink bottle on the paper where he had been practising the newly acquired art of writing. The one rushes to the corner for his rusty harpoon, relic of an early whaling voyage to Greenland. The other snatches the toysker ;* while the tyro in literature seizes a gun he had borrowed of a neighbour. *Pell-mell*, often shoeless and bareheaded they scamper to the beach, where numbers are already gathered, and are gathering every moment for the *melée*. What is it thus impels men to the hunt ? Its gain is questionable,— its dangers not improbable,—its fatigue undoubted. But emulation—activity—pursuit, seem natural to man ; indeed he only shares these impulses in common with all other animals. Revelation, reason, forbid it not. Therefore man is a hunter,—sometimes a mighty hunter—one we know was " a mighty hunter before the Lord."

The Shetlander, then, denied woods and prairies, rushes to *the sea*, whereon he may indulge this universal instinct, with all the zest and spirit of a " Melton" or " Caledonian" huntsman ; and we

---

* *Toysker*,—A huge sort of knife with which the turf is cut in oblong squares for fuel.

believe we may assure all who have not witnessed
it, without fear of contradiction from those who
have, that a Shetland hunt is quite equal in interest
and excitement to any other whatever, or whereso-
ever. The great difficulty or draw-back as we
have already said, is in the absence of due subordi-
nation, or even judicious co-operation among the
hunters. But suppose they act for mutual benefit
with a little common sense, the following is the
usual routine of the sport. First, there is a scramble for the boats on the beach, where private rights
seem for a time to be merged in "first come, first
served." The whales are seen in hundreds, plunging about in the midst of the bay or voe. The
mothers can be observed, chasing about and watching over the little ones with the greatest fondness,
while several sentinels a little apart, are on the
watch. The boats being launched and manned,
separately and as silently as possible, are rowed so as
to get between the herd and the open sea; some
remain there, while the rest begin to close in around
the poor wanderers, as yet probably unaware of
danger, and only congratulating themselves, that
after the heavy weather they had of late encount-
ered, they have now reached a sheltered and peaceful place for repose and refreshment; more boats
momently arrive, coming round the headlands from
neighbouring voes, whither the "fiery cross" has
also been carried. These are by this time most
acceptable assistants, as they serve to swell the
phalanx that bars the return of the prey to the
ocean. Perhaps, however, the whales are far too

numerous for any available force to manage *as a whole*. In this case the hunters are compelled to detach one wing of the vast army, which being tolerably well inclosed, the rest make off seaward, while many a wistful, longing look is cast after them. The animals appear to follow in detachments one larger and more powerful than the rest as a leader. The object then is, for some of the boats to get as close to *him* as is consistent with safety, if possible to shoot at, or harpoon him, or otherwise cause him to rush on his fate to the shore; which, when he finds himself wounded or beset, and getting into shallow water, he almost invariably does. This is the most difficult and dangerous part of the affair, and ought to be intrusted to the most skilful and experienced person present. But before the hunt is sufficiently far advanced for this to be accomplished, there commences a most extraordinary uproar. Each man engaged in the undertaking, lifts his voice in shouting, mingled with shrieks and howls, as loud and unearthly as possible,—the more demon-like the better, together with the rattle of any sounding metal, with which they have come duly prepared,—showers of stones, firing of muskets, and even tuneless violins. The intention of all which, is to alarm and intimidate the prey, too powerful still for their persecutors, did they but know it. This part of the proceeding occupies a considerable time, often some hours, perhaps even a night; and on a lovely summer's midnight, when every thing on land is sleeping quietly in the profound calm of "the dim," the uproar on the water has a most extraordinary effect. The whales, however, are rather obstinate; they decline being driven to their destruction, or, at least, will think twice or thrice about it first. Sometimes they seem to be taking counsel together,—sometimes they make a swift and desperate rush towards shore, when the noises are redoubled, with triumphant huzzas,—anon they turn, and attempt to force their way back, compelling the boats to retire a little space, when solemn silence suddenly ensues for a time. Sometimes the whales now escape in spite of every precaution; plunging downwards they find a passage beneath the boats, which it may be supposed are then in a critical position. Very few accidents, however, occur; for though occasionally a boat or two may get a capsize, help is so near, that some wet jackets is the amount of damage. In the more fortunate instances of complete success, the unruly prey is at length driven gradually to land. The patriarch leader receives several severe wounds, and in his agony, precipitates himself aground, when the whole herd follow headlong. The men, now close behind, leap into the water, and joined by more fresh hands, who have been waiting on the beach, in the utmost excitement and impatience, slaughter the poor whales with guns, knives, or any other weapon at hand. This is a terribly wholesale butchery, and to the spectator is the most disagreeable part of the proceedings. But the men are in the highest state of joyful excitement, thinking of nothing but how most quickly to secure the valuable spoil, ere the hours of darkness come on.

N

After a night of profound repose, well earned by their day's fatigues, the fishermen awake to the glad consciousness, that there is yet an agreeable part of the business before them, namely the division of the booty. They hasten therefore to the scene of yesterday's triumph. Every one who chased or assisted in the slaughter of the whales, is there himself, or by his proxy, probably a hundred, or a hundred and fifty men. The number of the whales is usually from three to seven or eight hundred. They are from twelve to twenty feet long, and are each worth about two pounds. Being counted, and valued according to size, by competent judges, a third of the whole is set aside for the proprietor of the ground on which they have been stranded; the rest are equally divided among the men. In general there are some monied or mercantile individuals present, who buy on the spot, at a venture, the shares of some of the hunters. Some transfer their's to their landlord, or his factor, against rent-day, while others choose to flinch and boil the blubber that falls to them for their own use. The carcases and bones are in too many instances suffered to lie on the beach as a nuisance, or are again committed to the sea; whereas, if the Shetlanders were as active and energetic in the agricultural line, as they are in the sea-faring, quantities of most valuable manure might be obtained from what is thus heedlessly wasted.

CHAPTER XVI.

THE EARLY PARTED.

ONE beautiful day, early in autumn, before harvest work in these northern regions had
commenced, a young and merry party crossed the
bleak hills of one of the remote Shetland Isles,
from the most northerly dwelling of man in Her
Majesty's dominions, towards the parish church,
for so is here the custom, to witness the ceremony
of marriage between two of their number.

The bride was a handsome girl in her nineteenth
year. She was in a simple dress of white,—white
shawl, white satin ribbons in her neat cap, and
the rather unusual finery for a cottage maid (a
present however) of white kid gloves. Her whole
appearance was strikingly prepossessing, and in
face, figure and demeanour, would, I thought, have
adorned a much higher station. Her bridegroom
was a few years older, and their courtship had
been even from the days of childhood.

Some circumstances had occurred to defer their
union for a few months beyond the time intended,
but at length they stood before the minister, who

was to join their lot in one.   Part of their landlord's family met them at church, to officiate as
bride's maid and groom's man; and the whole
party, including the son of a well known and much
respected ornament of the law in Edinburgh, who
happened to be on a visit to the Island, soon re-
traced their steps to the hyperborean cottage, to
spend the evening in dancing, and other amusements suitable to the occasion.   Healths were
pledged to the happiness of the youthful pair, of
course; but we rarely find intemperance sullying
such meetings in Shetland.   The newly united
couple were poor in worldly goods, but he was a
clever and adventurous fisherman, and she had
been brought up to be frugal and industrious; and
they had mutual love in strength and purity to
light them on their path through the world that
was before them.   So, after a few days, they repaired to their future home, in the cottage of the
bridegroom's father.

It was about the same time next year, I saw the
youthful mother, carry her first-born to church for
baptism.   Though a little paler than when she
stood in the same spot a bride, yet she looked all
the more interesting.   Once more she was in the
same white dress, and I marked the blush of modest
pride that flushed her cheek, as she sought and
caught *her father's* eye, while the name of *her
mother* was pronounced over her child.   The re-
sponsive tear trembled in my own eye, as I marked her's filling, and my heart echoed the prayer

that no doubt swelled in the young and happy parents' hearts.

Not many weeks afterwards, when the cheerful festivities of Christmas were just approaching, after many days of stormy unsettled weather, a calm lovely morning invited my favourite Agnes, to visit her own father's house, for the few short hours of daylight which this season affords. Every object was reflected in the calm bright mirror of the placid ocean, and the air was balmy as on a day in June. She took her child in her arms, and left her husband with his father and brother, engaged in some little work of husbandry on their small farm. She called to him cheerfully as she passed at a little distance, to come for her before the evening darkened, and he returned an affectionate assent. Alas! for the young hearts, *severed, then for ever!*

Very shortly after Agnes's departure, some of their neighbours proposed to go to the fishing, and two lads from a little distance arrived with their fishing tackle and bait. Without waiting for their usual boat-fellows, as the forenoon was advancing, the father and two sons I have mentioned, set off in company with another boat, to the fishing-ground, six miles off the north point of the land. They had nearly reached the spot, when a sudden storm arose; the tide was at the full, and the force of the North Atlantic rushed in with the speed of a whirlwind on the poor devoted crews. One of the boats was well manned, and reached the land

in safety; but in the little bark wherein was
Agnes's husband, he and his brother were the only
efficient hands,—their aged father and the two lads
above alluded to composing the rest of the crew.
They were never more heard of; the deep and
turbid ocean overwhelmed them ; and, till the day
when the sea shall give up the dead, *how* they met
their fate can never be known.

We shall draw a veil over the sorrows of the
heart-stricken survivors of this catastrophe,—the
aged and desolate woman, bereft of her husband
and both her sons,—a destitute widow and large
family of one of them,—a youthful betrothed bride
of one of the younger men,—a despairing mother
of the other, who had in him lost her only surviving stay, having, two years before, by a precisely
similar accident, had to mourn for husband, son,
and son-in-law,—and last, though not least, the
poor Agnes, on whose little story I have been
dwelling with melancholy interest. What were
her feelings when the fierce and sudden storm
arose, sweeping over the waste of waters she was
gazing on ? She believed her husband safe on
shore. First came to her ear reports that boats
were gone to sea. Who were in them ? When
the one boat arrived with the hardy crew utterly exhausted with the struggle for their lives, the alarm
was raised, and very shortly it became evident that
the other would never reach the land. The storm
subsided almost as rapidly as it had risen; but its
appointed work was accomplished, and under the

all-wise direction of the Ruler of wind and waves, it had summoned to His dread tribunal the souls of these poor fishermen.

Agnes remains in the dwelling of her father, of which she was the pride and joy, and where she is now not the less tenderly cherished, because of her irreparable misfortune

CHAPTER XVII.

THE SHIPWRECK.

IN the month of February, nearly thirty years ago, a fearful storm swept over the Shetland Islands. The gale commenced in the afternoon, from the south-east, increasing as the moonless night came on, and was accompanied with thick snow. No scene can be imagined more dreary than that which these islands present under such circumstances. The ocean spray mingled with the snow flakes, wraps sea, earth, and sky, in one desolating cloud, while the roar of the furious wind, and the thunder of the mighty breakers, combine to deafen the ears, and appal the hearts of those even most familiar with their sounds.

On such an evening, the Shetland peasant, after looking to the safety of his boat on the beach, and spreading a few handfuls of fodder before the shivering animals cowering near his cottage, would early close his door, and with his family prepare for a few hours of tranquil industry before rest. The father will then make or mend shoes for himself, or wife, or child; or assisted by his sons, he will manufacture the keyshies (straw baskets) for home use,—and the females card, spin, and knit, their fine wool. When midnight has passed, one light after another is extinguished in the lowly dwellings, and the inmates are buried in silence and repose. Doubtless many a wife and mother, on a night like that we have alluded to, would press a sleepless pillow, her fancy wandering to the absent sailor, perchance exposed to those wildly warring elements; but ere long, even these anxieties would be hushed in sleep, as the sea-boy at the mast-head, is said to be "lulled to rest by the rocking of the storm."

At this hour then, a stately ship was lying-to in the gale, in imagined safety, but really in dangerous proximity to the rocks of Shetland. She was bound from Hamburgh to New Orleans, with a valuable cargo. The captain had come on deck after a short repose, to look at the weather, and confident in the qualities of his ship, and the reckoning he had kept, supposing himself at least fifty miles to the northward of Shetland, with a free and open sea before him, he was about to " turn in " again, when the watch made the appalling cry,— " Breakers a-head ! "

" Call all hands on deck to wear the ship," was the instant and calm command.

But in a few minutes all was consternation, and then despair, as they perceived the vessel was driving before wind and sea, among the very breakers whose boom they had so lately first heard. Ere any measures could by possibility be adopted for averting the calamity, the noble bark struck heavily on the north point of a small uninhabited island stretching across the mouth of a snug yet spacious harbour, and thereby disabled her helm. Had the hapless mariners been acquainted with the particulars of their situation, and in circumstances to have taken advantage of them, a few hundred yards of a narrow but safe entrance, would have brought them to an anchorage, where they should have rode out the maddest hurricane in perfect security; but it was not so to be. The vessel, now beyond control of her helm, drifted onwards, across the entrance of the harbour, right in the face of a frowning mural precipice, that faced the east.

The supercargo, with his youthful new-wedded wife, rushed on deck in their night-dresses, just as the ship was dashed with resistless force on the precipitous headland, rebounded, and again striking, parted in two amidships. Clinging to each other in an agonizing embrace, and uttering one piercing cry for mercy on their souls, the young couple, with several passengers, and half of the crew, sunk with the hinder part of the vessel, and were seen no more! The fore-part, on which were the captain and the rest of the crew, was now drifted northwards, into what appeared to them the open sea, and they imagined they had only the fearful prospect of being carried helplessly past all chance of escape, and of perishing with cold and hunger, believing, as they did, that they had struck on the most northerly point of the land. Very soon, however, they were undeceived, and the remains of the unfortunate bark were shivered into fragments on another point, when eleven more human beings were hurried into an awful eternity.

On the top of the cliff, where the last fearful scene of this tragedy was enacted, yet sheltered by a bluff hill that rose behind it, stood a solitary cottage. So near was it to the rocky brink of the ravine or geo, that had the howlings of the storm been less loud, or had the senses of the inmates been less accustomed to those terrific blasts, they might have heard the anguished death-cries of the forty souls that perished that night. But the cottars all slept soundly, the sleep earned by toil, and sweetened by minds at peace. The lowly hut was wrapped in the drifting snow, and no friendly light glimmered from its little window, yet thither the good hand of Providence guided a shivering and desolate stranger.

The Shetland peasant's door is never barred, nor is any demand on his hospitality grudgingly answered. A dripping, bruised, and half-dead sailor, was therefore instantly admitted to the fisherman's dwelling, though he avowed it was with mistrustful trembling he committed himself thus to the power of strangers; for he had heard wild tales of cruel wreckers, who would murder survivors, for the sake of plundering the vessel stranded on their coasts. He wronged deeply, however, the simple and kindly Shetlanders by the suspicion; for whatever may be their ignorant deductions as to the right of wrecked property, a suffering fellow-creature, especially a seaman,

never receives at their hands ought but tender
compassion and assistance. So the sleeping embers were stirred up, fresh turf was heaped on the
hearth, and dry clothes, and warmed milk procured for the stranger, who then, and afterwards,
poor fellow, expressed his thankfulness and gratitude in the most affecting terms.

As soon as the melancholy morning dawned, a
messenger was sent to the fisherman's landlord, who
was also the nearest justice of peace, before whom,
therefore, the shipwrecked man wished to make
the necessary official declarations. The snow was
falling thick, and the gale continuing, but the laird
sent a pony and his servant, to bring the stranger
to his house, where medical assistance, and every
comfort was afforded that the situation of the forlorn one required; and after a sojourn of some
weeks, he was enabled to return to his country.
To his host he narrated, in a manly, yet modest
strain, the history of his wonderful escape.

He was the master and sole survivor of the unfortunate vessel, a pleasing, intelligent, and very
handsome man about thirty years of age. He was
a native of Norway, but spoke English fluently.
When the vessel had gone to pieces he was clinging
to the mast, along with which he was repeatedly
dashed upon the rocks, and then washed off by the
succeeding wave. He was frequently compelled to
dive to clear himself from the floating fragments of
wood and tackling, yet he preserved wonderful
courage and self-possession ; so that, finding his
jacket and boots impeded his exertions, he seated

himself on the mast and calmly disencumbered himself of them; then recollecting, according to the common belief of seafaring people, that every third wave is always the highest, he watched attentively for this fortunate billow, which at length threw him so far onwards on the the rocky beach, whither the remains of the wreck were now drifted, that exerting all his strength he secured his footing, and was able to crawl on hands and knees beyond the reach of the next succeeding wave; here in a crevice of the rock he rested a little, the sea spray and snow almost smothering him, yet still collected and undaunted. At length he managed, bruised and stiff as he was, to scramble up a bank of steep broken rocks, and after half an hour's miserable wandering, he discovered the lowly, but hospitable cottage we mentioned. To his own coolness and courage, under God, he owed his life, and he averred that amidst all the horrors that surrounded him, he felt confident he should be saved. He had been at sea ever since his early boyhood,—this was his second shipwreck, and he felt sure he should never be drowned.

On being repeatedly asked his reasons for this confident persuasion, he at length gave the following account.

He had been married for a few months to a beautiful girl, to whom he was much attached. The ship was laden and cleared out, and only waited a favouring breeze for sailing, which seemed now to have arrived,—and the captain and his wife were seated at breakfast. The young woman, oppressed with the idea of the approaching parting, stole many a hurried glance at her husband, but dared not trust her eye to meet his, lest her assumed composure should fail her. He soon started up, "well Carolina, cheer up now! the wind is really favourable and seems steady; I shall soon be summoned to go on board."

Carolina burst into tears.

"Well Olaf, you will go, and I shall never see you more," she sobbed.

"Pooh, pooh, Carolina, is this your promised fortitude?" remonstrated her husband.

"Nay, but just hear me dear," said poor Carolina, "I had such a dream last night, and God knows, many such I shall have during your absence; I am sure something is to happen to you,—and we shall meet no more!" she added weeping passionately,

"Now this is ever the way with you women" said the sailor, his voice faltering however, "you would try to unman the bravest heart with your dreamings and your fears: let not my Carolina be so silly."

"Well husband I will not" said Carolina checking her sobs, "if you will grant me one favour. There is an old woman who lives not far from this who can tell the future most surely,—come and let us ask her about this voyage which to me appears ill-omened; and if she says you are not to return, go with you yet, I will, and share your fate!"

"As to your going, Carolina, with me to sea, that is out of the question, for many good reasons, but if it will please you, I will accompany you to this

weird woman ;" and a seaman's proverbial superstition stole over him, unconsciously lending weight
to his desire of soothing his timid and endeared companion. So the pair muffled themselves close up,
and proceeded hastily and in silence to a miserable
abode, in the most miserable quarter of the old
town of Hamburgh. Carolina knocked softly at a
door. She had visited the old woman's dwelling
ere now. She had asked her of the fate of her absent betrothed one, and having been told that he
would soon return from a prosperous voyage, and
be united to her, and this prediction having been
duly fulfilled, Carolina now firmly believed she
should again receive a truthful prophecy, and thus
either have her forebodings removed, or know the
worst at once. While these thoughts chased each
other through her mind, a pleasing looking, but
very meanly clad young woman, admitted the
captain and his wife to a dismal passage, and this
led them down to a large, dark apartment, with
bare damp walls, earthen floor, and a low fire on a
miserable hearth, round which three flat stones
were placed, as the only seats. On one of them
was the old sibyl, who desiring her visitors to be
seated likewise, scanned them earnestly by the dim
fire-light to which her own optics were doubtless
accustomed, but which seemed to them, only to
" render the darkness visible." After a short silence
the ancient crone said slowly, "and what question
dost thou wish to put to me young *frau?*"

"My husband goes on a long sea-voyage,—will
he return in safety ?" said the silvery voice of

Carolina, which sounded like *a Sabbath-bell in Pandemonium*, if we could but imagine such a thing there. It was the simile of a doting husband.

The old woman rose and went to the farther corner of the apartment, where, by a rushlight she seemed to consult a page of an ancient volume. In a few moments she returned, and thus delivered her oracular response.

" The voyage of your husband will be a disastrous one; nevertheless, he will return safe and well; and what is more, *he will never die by drowning!*"

They left the wretched cellar, Carolina clinging more closely to her husband's arm, thankful for the equivocal, yet, on the whole, comforting assurance she had received, and in an hour afterwards she parted from him with tolerable composure.

And often, during the midnight storm, when startled from her troubled sleep by the sounds ever so fearful to the ear of the sailor's wife, she has composed herself to rest again, murmuring,— " He will never die by drowning."

Alas! poor Captain H——, and his affectionate Carolina, like many others, were doomed to experience the futility,—the worse than folly,—of such dependance.

On his next voyage, in the following year, his vessel foundered at sea, and he was heard of no more!

But to return to the scene of the shipwreck in Shetland. The news of the disaster spread like wildfire, and notwithstanding the inclemency of the weather, most of the inhabitants of the neighbouring district of the island, which was a comparatively populous one, hurried to the spot, as soon as it was light.

Just round the point where the captain had been cast ashore, was a small open bay or *wick*, with a low pebbly beach, and each tremendous billow, as it rolled before the still thundering gale, was bearing with it bales and boxes of valuable property,—linen and lace forming the chief parts of the cargo,—together with the wood of the wreck, always a most acceptable commodity to the Shetlander.

Now it is nearly a hopeless task to attempt to convince these islanders,—and they are not singular in this unhappy delusion,—that what is tossed at the mercy of the all-devouring sea, can be of right the property of any but those who are able to rescue it from certain destruction. Accordingly, men, and even women, waded into the dangerous surf, braving wind and snow, and sea, to secure for themselves the wealth they saw before them,—boxes of jewellery and tea,—wearing apparel, and every article so large a vessel would necessarily require, besides the cargo, were strewn in profusion on the shore. Sometimes, alas! the bodies of the drowned were disentangled from the heaps. Increasing crowds increased only the number of plunderers. Every thing was carried off that was sufficiently portable.

The weather was so fearful, and every one was so much occupied, that it was some hours ere the magistrate was aware of what was going on, or could procure a few stout men to act as special

constables under his directions for the protection
of the wrecked property. At length, however, this
was accomplished, and these men prevailed on a
few of those they found at the beach, to join with
them in saving some of the most unwieldy bales, and
the largest pieces of the wreck. These they collected, and mounted guard over the pile,—and this was
the amount of the assistance they could render.
Some still more distressing features were added to
the picture in the course of the day, short and drear,
and sad as it was. Among the other things cast
on shore, there were several casks of spirits, of
which the people partook, chiefly as a preventive
against cold and exhaustion, though a few were
more incautious, and two persons paid for this a
melancholy penalty. One man perished by falling
into a snow wreath on his way to his more distant
home, and another died from cold and intemperance,
and was found by his wife in the morning, close to
his own dwelling, laden with the spoil for which he
paid so dear.

The wind sank during the night, and was succeeded by an intense and bitter frost, and next day
the sun rose unclouded on the brightness of the
snow, and the still labouring sea, which was rolling
in with every huge but rapidly subsiding wave, the
spoil that yet floated on the waters of the little bay.

The inhabitants of the more remote parts of the
island, now hastened for a share of the plunder,
and as it was not so plentiful as on the preceding
day, no little contention took place, the unbridled
passions of cupidity and envy, being aggravated

by disappointment in some instances, and intoxi-
cation in others. The heap that the appointed
constables had charge of, was even attacked in their
madness.

The laird and some of his friends now thought
it might be wise in them to repair to the scene of
action, and a striking one it was,—one perhaps
never to be witnessed in civilized Britain except
here, and not even here since the days of "the
Pirate Cleveland;" and be it remembered this is no
fiction, but an unvarnished narrative of an actual
occurrence.

The beach was thronged with men, women, and
children. The purity of the driven snow was
trampled and sullied by many footsteps, rarely to
be seen in that lonely spot. The most mighty of
nature's elements was vividly displaying its triumphs
over the most majestic work of human art,—and
man's demon-like passions seemed as if mocking
the very wrath of heaven,—while

"The sun looked smiling bright
On the wild and woeful sight."

The magistrate's first act, was to order the
spirit-casks to be staved; and then as a measure
of intimidation, and in their own self-defence, he
armed his constables with such weapons as he could
collect.

An express was sent as soon as the weather
would permit a boat to cross out of the island, to
the coast guard officers, and the Custom-house at
Lerwick, but this was fifty miles distant, and no
help was nearer at hand.

The magistrate exerted all his influence to check the depredations he witnessed. In vain did he tell the people there was one man saved, to whom the property belonged as representative.

"Nae doot, Sir, nae doot honest man, let him come and tak all he can. None here shall stop him !"

In vain were they assured that if they would save what they could for the owners or underwriters, they would be liberally rewarded.

"Vera true, Sir," was the respectful reply, "but then, Sir, ye see, them that hardly lifts a finger, would get share and share alike wi' us, that perils life and health in the cause ; na, na, sir. The sea sends us a blessing, and we'll just tak it as it comes, and be thankful."

Here was a case where "might made right." The lawless ones numbered twenty to one of the better principled. Yet the brave and powerful men appointed to watch over the valuable heap that had been saved, by their firmness and forbearance maintained their charge through another bitter night ; and ere the third had set in, Custom-house officers and other authorities had arrived.

A rigorous search now took place in the neighbouring houses, and in the dwellings of those persons who had been recognised among the plunderers. Only in a very few instances however were some trifles recovered. In the thatch of the cottages, in the snow wreaths among the hills, buried in the yards and fields, or even anchored off in some lonely geo in the bosom of the very ele-

ment from which it had been so lately rescued,—
much valuable property was concealed and afterwards secured little injured.

For months, nay years afterwards, these ill
gotten goods might be seen in every cottage, not
only in the island where the wreck took place, but
in many others over Shetland, having been hawked
about by travelling pedlars, and otherwise given
or bartered among the people. It was great wealth
to those who are little accustomed to any addition
to their usual scanty means ; but it proved, (as "ill
gotten gear" so often does,) quite as great a curse
as a blessing, as it undoubtedly first gave many of
the islanders a taste for luxuries to which their
ordinary resources are inadequate, but which they
still crave after, and often improvidently endeavour
to procure.

But it may very naturally be asked,—Are the
Shetlanders still no more enlightened? Are they
no better instructed on the subject of wrecks than
they were thirty years ago? Would a scene like
that described now take place under similar circumstances? No doubt the progress of universal
improvement has reached even here, to a certain
extent; yet still are these islands isolated, still
forgotten or overlooked, and in many things un-
pardonably neglected. The laws are very negli-
gently enforced, private grievances are with difficulty, or not at all, redressed. Religious instruction is, for the most part, very sparingly and
grudgingly bestowed, so that while the social condition of the people is in many respects ameliorated,

ancient mistakes, superstitions, and delusions, keep hold of their minds, and we fear, influence, and will influence, their conduct; and although nothing amounting to the same temptation, or on a similar scale, has occurred since the wreck above described, there are few seasons in which the shores are not strewed with fragments of some sort, which are appropriated, without compunction, by all who find them.

But the chief and very sufficient reason why wrecked property is so little respected in these islands, is the niggardly amount of salvage the law allows to those who exert themselves, even to endangering life, in saving from the boisterous breakers a part of their prey. Until some more just system of remuneration is adopted, we fear the Shetlanders will still "just tak the blessing" from the deep, forgetful of, or disregarding the Crown, or any other dues, excepting those connected with self-interest.

CHAPTER XVIII.

THE SUNKEN ROCK.

IT is now a good many years ago, that a number of persons, fifteen or twenty at least, went to Lerwick in a large boat from a distant island, to exchange, as is usual, their hose, butter, feathers, &c., for other articles they stood in need of. There were a bride and bridegroom, who had gone to purchase necessaries for their approaching wedding ; there were also husbands and wives, and several young women, together with the boatmen.

Having finished their business in the town, they were just embarking to return, when a man and his wife, with several children, who had all been many years abroad, asked and obtained permission to share their passage.

They left Lerwick on a fine winter morning. Christmas was near at hand, and they were all,— not least the long absent,—anxious to reach their homes, that they might "make merry and be glad," with their friends, on the fruits of their honest industry. The boat was heavily laden, but the sea was smooth, and the light wind favourable. One of the men had a violin, and they beguiled their ten hours sail with music and song, and innocent mirth,—so at least it was reported.

Evening came; there was no moon, but a clear, dark-blue sky, bespangled with night's living gems. The voyagers had reached the nearer shore of the island they were bound for, and coasting along, had only one point of land to turn, ere they would be in the snug harbour they sought.

Alas! alas! they never reached that harbour! Not one appeared to tell the sad tale.

Their friends were under no apprehensions at their non-appearance for several days, so fine was the weather. They supposed that something had occurred to detain them. But by the arrival of some other persons, it was found, that they had left the town early on the morning of the fatal day. Then some individuals who lived near to the shore the boat had to pass, recollected that about eight o'clock that evening, they heard, as it were, distant cries, but had no suspicion at the time whence they came; nor if they had, could they have rendered any timely assistance.

There was,—there is,—a dangerous SUNKEN ROCK on the coast, which the hapless boat must have incautiously approached, and struck on in the darkness. Search was accordingly made along the beach in that direction, where there were found some pieces of the boat, with light trunks and packages, which too plainly told the fate of the unfortunate voyagers.

But what, will it be supposed was farther found? Not a body washed on shore,—for the wind had

since blown off the land, and carried every thing
out to sea, except a very few light articles which
the tide had at first wafted in. But there was
found, above the high-water mark, seated on a
stone, leaning up along the overhanging bank, a
little child of three years old! Its cherub head
rested on one hand, and a piece of bread was in
the other, which lay in its lap. It was comfortably wrapped up, and its countenance perfectly
placid, as if asleep; but of course it was dead!

Imagination lingers to ask—How came it there?
Did it suffer long? Or, were its pangs mercifully
shortened? Oh, who can tell! But it was con-
jectured, that as the father was an excellent swim-
mer, when the accident happened, he had gained
the shore with this his pet little girl, who, when
they left the town, had been seated on his knee,
and having placed her, as he deemed in safety, he
had returned to try to save some more of his family,
and had perished with them all.

And this was the return of the exile to his
fatherland,—this the melancholy disappointment to
his expecting relatives,—this the mournful relic of
the yearningly longed-for little family, at the aged
grandsire's hearth.

CHAPTER XIX.

NORNA.

THERE died not long ago, in one of these islands, a singular character, who might have sat for the portrait of Norna of Fitful Head; though the web of mystery and sorrow which the "Great Magician" interwove with the history of the latter, is here wanting.

Suneva Renton laid claim to the character of a "wise woman," skilled in medicine and occult science; but especially to the gifts said to be conferred by "Fairy Folk." A midwife by profession, she possessed the reputation of undoubted, unfailing skill, exercised, however, too often without the least spark of human sympathies or kindliness. Self-reliance and decision she displayed in abundance, and her experience was unquestionable; and by these she acquired among her countrywomen, and country-men too, if truth must be told, a very singular degree of influence, so that she was consulted till her death, in all sorts of mysterious diseases, or what to the common people appeared such, and that in animals as well as in human beings. But these applications to the

" wise woman" were carefully concealed whenever
it was possible; and it was a laughable circumstance, that as her nearest neighbour was the minister, whom she considered her worst enemy, persons from distant islands who came to seek her
assistance, on inquiring the way to her residence,
asked, to deceive the informant, for *the Manse*,
which they as invariably passed to go to the next
cottage.

Mother Suneva's knowledge of herbs and simples
was extensive, and her applications of them were
correct and judicious, which, no doubt, contributed
much to her success and reputation; but her
charms and incantations were at least as often in
request, and more firmly relied on. For example,
if a pony were laid aside, in midst of its work, by
spavin, she would tie a twisted woollen thread,
spun by herself with various spells, round the animal's body, and turn him loose to the hill. For a
few days he must *not be looked at*,—or the charm
was broken,—and then he would be found completely cured.

She was a woman of great strength of body, as
well as mind; of much natural shrewdness also,
and sagacity; and she stated her pretensions with
a confidence of asseveration,—a superiority of language, and a loftiness of manner, which might have
indeed befitted her of the Fitful Head, and which
easily made her way to the credulity of her equals
in birth and education, and left her superiors in
doubt, whether she were not herself deceived.

With little of the "milk of human kindness" in

her bosom, she ruled her large family, and even her husband, with a rod of iron, and was by them respected and obeyed, with an alacrity and zeal, rarely witnessed in Shetland families of their class, where parental love is exemplary, but filial duty too little cultivated.

The following is our heroine's own account of some of her interviews with the "wise people," and the gifts she received from them. She was sitting alone, on a calm, hazy, summer's day, when a man, extremely good-looking, and about thirty years of age, came in, and said, "A woman required her services immediately." She got up and followed him, as soon as she had thrown her shawl around her. She then asked who the person was to whom she was going, but he replied, she would soon see that. In what appeared a very brief space of time, she came to a place she had never seen, and wondered much how such a house had arisen, so near her own residence, without her knowledge. When she entered the house, which was much superior to those she was accustomed to, she met a cousin of her own, whom she had not seen for years, but believed to be dead, and she used the common exclamation, " Gude be near us ! Andrew, is this you?" He instantly enjoined her on no account to use *the holy name* there ; and as she valued her life and salvation, not to eat or drink, since then, no evil should harm, or power be of avail to detain her. She was very soon summoned to her patient, and in due time a beautiful young wife was safely delivered of a fair and promising

" lad bairn." The man who came for her now
brought what appeared to be wine or brandy, and
bread, but she steadily refused the offered refreshment ; and having given to a female attendant the
necessary directions for the treatment of the
mother and babe, she proposed to depart. Her
cousin led her out, and at the door she found her
own pony saddled for her use. The same person
accompanied her to her home, and it was night ere
she reached it, shivering, hungry, and weary.

On another occasion our favoured acquaintance
was travelling alone to visit one of her family who
lived at a little distance, when a man like the
former met her, and asked her advice respecting
some complaint wherewith his wife was afflicted.
She told him clearly and promptly what to do, and
he requested that she would meet him in the same
place in eight days. Thither accordingly mother
Suneva repaired, and found the same person waiting her. He informed her his wife was so much
the better of the advice he had received, as to be
nearly quite well. He said he could not reward
her with money, since *his* would prove of no use to
her ; but he hung a hair chain around her neck,
and assured her she was under the protection of
those who could and would assist and befriend
her in every undertaking, and that no case of suffering or sickness which she conducted would ever
fail of success. Accordingly in touching with an
ancient coin for scrofula, " telling away" sprains
and bruises in man and beast, as well as curing all
diseases incident to both, foretelling the future,

and guarding against accidents, she was without a rival, and is now, so far as we are aware, without a successor. We would fain hope the day is past, for other Norna's to arise, even in these remote and neglected isles.

To the above sketch of this singular individual, it may be added, that she was very handsome, indeed a beautiful woman, of majestic height and fine proportions. She had large piercing and intelligent dark eyes; in her youth her hair was raven black, and her complexion rich and glowing. Her last, indeed only illness, was that of old age; for though she had not exceeded the ordinary allotted span of human existence, her constitution was worn down by the fatigue and exposure incident to her mode of life. Her religious views, strange to say, were singularly correct and evangelical *in theory*,—in practice she was too much of the pharisee. Not a doctrine, or a duty, or a sentiment could be mentioned in her hearing, but she knew,—had practised, or responded to it. She retained the full possession of all her faculties, and the last breath that trembled on her lips, was an aspiration for *mercy*,—not unnecessarily surely, if we consider the delusions she practised so long and so undauntedly, and the evils arising to the deceived votaries whom she misled to believe and confide in them.

CHAPTER XX.

A SHETLAND LOCHINVAR.

THE custom of betrothal, it is well known, is a
very ancient one, and is still practised in
Germany, and in the East; though in the British
Isles, we believe, it is extinct, except in some remote districts of Ireland, and in the primitive
Islands of Shetland. In the former mentioned
countries, a couple intending themselves or intended by their parents or guardians to unite in
marriage, the design is signified to the assembled
friends and relatives, when rings and other gifts
are exchanged, and feasting and congratulations
anticipate the future joy. This may take place
weeks or months, or even many years, before the
matrimonial union. Originally the ceremony of
betrothal was intended to be as binding as the
marriage vow, and might be infringed with as little
impunity. Hence arose the dilemma of Joseph,
the carpenter of Nazareth, with respect to his
" espoused" (betrothed), but not married " wife"—
the virgin mother of our Lord. Hence also the
espousal or betrothal of Isaac to Rebecca, by the
mission of Abraham's servant, and the gifts of

jewels to her. And our readers will at once recol-
lect, that one of Sir Walter Scott's delightful
fictions was founded on a similar circumstance.

In the obligatory nature of the engagement
entered into at betrothal, except in so far as any
other promise is in honour binding, the common
custom still retained in Shetland, does not involve
the parties. It is thus conducted :—

On the Saturday evening previous to the marriage, which latter is in almost all cases on Thursday,
the bridegroom accompanied by his chief grooms-
man (*best* man, he is here called,) after giving in
the names to the clerk for proclamation next day,
repairs to the home of the bride, where all the immediate relatives of both parties have been invited
to a special feast. A social meeting and drinking
of healths and *good luck* to the contracting pair, is
all the ceremonial ; but this is called the "contract,"
and in practice, though not in law, the parties are
considered bound to each other ; they are called
"*half married*." The bride remains in strict
seclusion till the wedding day, and in very few instances, (though a few there have been,) are the
proceedings of the bridal subsequently stopped, yea,
though five days intervene, and " there is often
much between the cup and the lip" ;—witness the
following curious incident which took place not
many years ago.

The borders of one of the longest, and most
solitary voes in Shetland, is the scene of our story.
The adjacent hills were covered with dark peat
moss, and sloped pretty steeply down to the edge

of the sea. At the head of the voe, just where a
rapid brook found its way through an expanse of
silvery sand, to mingle with the waters of the
ocean, whose winter waves often swelled the little
streamlet with its briny flood for a considerable
distance inland, stood two or three cottages, with
a few patches of cultivated land. All the rest of
the scenery was drear and bleak. A stone's cast
from the cottages, several boats were drawn up on
the beach; they were surrounded by a low dyke
of rough stones, and within this slight inclosure
(or boat-noost, as it is called), on one occasion stood
a pair of youthful lovers. They had grown up
from childhood together, but their course of love
was "not to run smooth." The maiden was
fair and very gentle; she was naturally shy,
silent, and reserved,—although she loved deeply
and well, with all the purity and exclusiveness of
woman's first attachment. Her father was what
is called, for a Shetland fisherman, "well to do,"
and he brought up his family to be careful and industrious. He had a few cattle and ponies, and a
fair stock of sheep on the neighbouring hills, so
that as his fishing paid the rent, he generally contrived about reckoning time, to have an additional
trifle to add to the little hoard in his landlord's
hands. The young man's connections, on the
contrary, were thriftless and unsteady; and this,—
the youngest surviving son,—was about to follow
two others, who had gone abroad as seamen.
Jamie, it might be thought, had an endearing tie
to his birth-place in the young girl, whose hand

was so closely clasped in his; and yet it seemed
all too soft and fragile to restrain his restless desire of desultory rambling, especially when the
well understood objections of the maiden's family
to their union were considered. So on that still
spring evening, with the holy stars above, the only
witnesses of their tryst, Jamie and Enga parted.
Jamie vowed eternal fealty, and swift return.
Enga said not a word, but probably she felt only
the more deeply.

Several years passed, during which Enga never
heard of or from her absent lover. This is unfortunately an occurrence too common in Shetland
families, to cause much surprise, but to Enga it did
occasion a tender and lasting regret. Diffident and
self-renouncing, she could only surmise, that if
Jamie lived, he had forgotten his early love. Now
Enga had several wooers. Her parents were
worldly wise; and after the most ancient and approved method of cruel parents, endeavoured to
persuade their daughter, that her lover was false,—
was dead,—was, in short, no longer to be thought
of, and that she must forthwith marry another, a
much richer and steadier, though sooth to say, less
lovable bridegroom.

Enga was persuaded, over persuaded,—it matters
not how. Whisper it not to the stars,—guardian
spirits of faith and love !—but pity and defend the
reluctant, yet at length tamely acquiescent bride.

The simple arrangements for the wedding were
finished, and the *contract* day arrived. A goodly
assemblage of guests had met, for whom abundant

cheer was provided by the self-satisfied approving father. The mother bustled hospitably,—sisters dressed and smiled,—brothers were boisterously merry,—and all were bright and gladsome, *but one!* A bride, indeed, is not expected to be gay, but Enga did not seem even quietly happy. She was pale and abstracted, and, it must be allowed, felt not quite satisfied that she was acting rightly; but she remained calm, till her father, in asking a blessing on the food, added a few words of prayer, that the intended nuptials might be happy and prosperous. Precious are the tears, which suppressed under the observation of our fellow-creatures, are poured forth freely at our Heavenly Father's footstool; and Enga turned aside to wipe such relieving drops from her cheek, while her grandmother muttered an old Shetland *saw*, which says—

> " Threaten'd love and thrawn kiss,
> Never deservéd wedded bliss."

The first cup of tea had been taken. This refreshment is here made a meal of, and is lingered over for some time, the knitting-needles always plying busily the while. During the interval that followed, when conversation had become general, a slight signal from a serving-girl, near the door, drew Enga's attention. Internally wondering for what purpose she could possibly be wanted on that occasion, yet glad to escape from observation for a time, the bride stole out. A young man, with whom she was acquainted, met her near the door-way, and saying there was a person at hand who wished to speak a word to her, he led her towards the sea-beach.

It was a murky evening in mid-winter; a drizzling rain was driven by the sighing wind into mist again, and Enga shivered as she felt the cold damp of the air, in contrast with the cheerful light and heated atmosphere she had left. But in one instant all this was unthought of, as she found a manly arm encircle her, and heard a voice she fancied she ought to know, whisper tremblingly, " Is it to find my Enga the bride of another I am come ?"

The poor girl, in pitiable bewilderment, could only gasp forth, she thought he never would come back.

" It is not yet too late," was the hurried rejoinder. " Will you come with me, my first, my only love ?"

A willing, yet modest affirmative was hardly spoken ere she was hurried off, between her old lover and his companion. They came to the " boat-noost," the trysting place where they had parted, and each, as they remembered the scene, pressed closer to the other,—sacred memories of youth's spring-time obliterating all that seemed harsh or doubtful in each other's conduct during the interval. A boat lay ready afloat, and into it the men helped the young woman, and pushed off. The light bark shot into the water, and rocked fearfully in the rising surge. Little recked the daring party that the tide was running strong,—that heavy gusts of wind were rushing down the gullies of the ad-

jacent hills, the indications of an approaching storm ;
while the booming thunder of the open ocean on the
other side of the opposite promontory, told in un-
mistakable tones of danger,—and how often on
those wild shores—of death ! In defiance of all this,
however, the men hoisted the close-reefed square-
sail of the skiff. Jamie took the helm and the
sheet-rope in either hand. Andrew, his friend,
stood by the halyard at the mast, and Enga trembling, yet unshrinking, seated herself at her lover's
feet. During the next hour of this rash and
dangerous voyage not a word was uttered, except
once or twice a whisper of encouragement or en-
dearment from Jamie to his stolen bride. The men
were too well acquainted with their duty in the
management of their boat, and too intent on its
judicious performance for conversation, or even
remark ; and truly on that night, their task
tested to the utmost all their courage, as well as
dexterity.

They had hardly commenced their voyage down
the long irregular voe, when the wind rapidly
increased, but as it did so the sky became first clear,
and then illuminated with that most beautiful, but
most fearful of all atmospheric phenomena, the
aurora borealis,—fearful, because in Shetland it is
always observed to foretell, or accompany the most
stormy weather. This singular phenomenon, of
which science has not yet been able to afford a
satisfactory solution, presents in these islands, during
the autumn and winter months, a most extraordinary and beautiful appearance ; yet while it lightens

the otherwise dull and gloomy sky, the peasantry regard it with dread and superstition, probably on account of the scenes of storm and shipwreck, with which it has to them become associated.

At present, while Enga covered her eyes, her companions hailed the flashing coruscations, which enabled them to steer their boat more safely through the angry waters, over which she flew " like a thing of life," bearing the fate of brave and devoted hearts.

The sea spray often broke in clouds over the defenceless trio, and sometimes a more heavy gust than usual, would oblige Andrew suddenly to lower the sail a little, when the boat would pause and shiver like a startled steed, and anon, again commence its mad career. There was a point of land jutting out into the voe, where it made an abrupt bend, and for this the men anxiously watched, as the current there ran stronger, the eddy fiercer,— but the little cape once rounded, they would be in safety. Ere the mariners imagined they could by possibility have advanced so far, they found themselves close to the point, and ere any precautionary measures could be adopted, the sail suddenly flapped back ; the meeting stream of tide whirled the little bark about, and in another instant all had been over had not the sail been instantly lowered once again, and then a dexterous turn of the helm sent the brave and buoyant vessel safely round the point of danger, after a fearful stagger, indeed, almost a plunge into the boiling tide-way. During that terrific moment of suspense, the poor bride gave one suppressed and bitter scream, but Jamie said firmly, "courage love, trust in me, and sit still;" she did so, for his voice re-assured her, and in moments of deadly peril, women are often steady and cool as the bravest man. The dangerous crisis past, the voyagers found themselves running before a fair wind, and with a comparatively smooth sea, into a sheltered and romantic creek, and Enga with trusting helpfulness, could now bale out the water that had half filled their little skiff. A sail of ten minutes more, and then a light on shore welcomed the party to the dwelling they were bound for, which was that of the schoolmaster, and parish clerk. Here they landed thoroughly wet and stiff with cold, and here Enga may be said to have first *seen* her returned lover. He was imbrowned and older looking of course, than when she looked on him last, but his eye was as kind, his smile as cheery as ever, and Enga's heart was satisfied. She now learnt that Jamie had reached his native shore only the day previous, and by mere accident met an old neighbour, who informed him that Enga was on the very eve of marriage. Without one moment's delay he set off, hoping to be *in time*, but hardly daring to anticipate that first love would be triumphant; "yet I thought I knew your heart, Enga, and I *trusted* it," said he. The young people were warmed and refreshed at the school-house, and ere they left it, Enga's destiny was changed, by substituting her *first* for her *late* lover's name in the proclamation formula for the following day. After an hour's rest, and Enga had been more suitably wrapped up by her friend's care, the travellers again set forth on foot for a walk of several miles over a moorland hill, so that it was considerably past midnight when the returned sailor stood with his dearly won bride at his own father's door. The welcome which the runaway pair received, the warm hearts that surround many a humble Shetland fireside, could better imagine than we can describe. Ere Jamie sought his couch, he told the story of his wanderings, and accounted for his friends not having heard from him. It was partly because, with the uncalculating, but romantic dreaming of a sailor, he maintained the constant intention of returning to them with a surprise, and partly because not being able himself to write, he could only send home one or two messages and tokens, which never reached them. Finally, he told that having won both honour and competence, he meant to devote his future life to his faithfully loved Enga, whom he had so nearly lost. And then, indeed, she blushed and smiled, as a happy bride ought.

While our Shetland Lochinvar was thus gallantly bearing off the prize, to which indeed he was but justly entitled, what a scene took place at the home she had so precipitately left! It was, of course, not long ere the fair bride was missed from the company; but believing that some of the young men present had colluded to hide her from her careless maidens, according to old established sport on similar occasions, her female friends began jestingly to seek her, in every

likely and unlikely place. The jest ere long grew
into sad earnest.

" They sought her that night, and they sought her next day."

And her mother calling to mind the poor girl's
pale and pensive aspect, admitted only the horror-
inspiring idea, that she must have hidden her sorrows in the deep sea, and under this impression,
would not be withdrawn from the neighbouring
cliff, expecting there to find, at least, the floating
corpse of her they so despairingly sought. This
distraction lasted till some of the neighbours returned from the distant church on the ensuing
day, when to the unutterable and joyful surprise of
her relatives they were informed, that Jamie Smith
and Enga had been proclaimed three times during
divine service, and no objections being offered,
were seen afterwards to approach the session-
house, with one or two friends, where it was understood they were lawfully married by the clergyman.

The quondam " craven bridegroom" had been
from the first, the most composed of the party, respecting all that took place. Perhaps he was conscious he would have received a cold, reluctant
hand. Perhaps his motives had been all along
dictated more by interest than by exclusive affection. Perhaps it was merely that he was naturally of an easy indifferent temper. However this
may have been, his philosophy, when the whole
facts of the case became known, deserves to be re-
corded for an example to any,—we would fain

hope the instances are few,—who may be called to suffer in similar circumstances. "Let her be going," said he, "they're as gude fish in the sea as ever came oot o' it." And to this characteristic remark, we shall only add the gratifying information, that Jamie and Enga still live, and love each other devotedly as ever.

CHAPTER XXI.

MUNESS CASTLE.

EXCEPT the Burghs,* there are very few remains of antiquity in these islands. On a hill in Unst, is an ancient Scandinavian monument, consisting of three concentric circles of rough stones, most of them now buried under turf. This is one of the places where the solemn councils or law courts of the NORTHMEN were held.

About two miles nearer the sea is a heap of stones or *cairn*, such as is common enough in the Scottish Highlands, called *Harold's Grave*. On such a cairn, in Scotland, each passer by throws an additional stone, as a pious mark of respect to the memory of the hero or unfortunate, who sleeps below. But in Unst the grave of Harold is situated in a lonely spot near the top of a hill, and far removed from the haunts of men. Who this Harold was, is not known. A bay, that may be seen from the grave, is called *Haroldswick*.† Doubt-

---

* Here called "Broghs,"—the *gh* gutteral, as in the Scottish Lochs."

† *Wick*, in the Norse, means an open bay or harbour.

less some renowned *Viking** first landed here, and
probably met a violent death in one of the sudden
quarrels that often took place among these rovers
and their followers.

Of a date nearer to our own times, we find, in the
different islands, the remains of numerous old
chapels.   In every parish there are from three to
seven or eight, the locality still retaining the names
of the old saints or heroes to whose honour they
were dedicated.   Some of them seem to have been
beautifully constructed, and others are very small,
but as no care has been taken to preserve them
from spoliation, they have now, in many places
nearly disappeared, the surrounding grave-yards
alone pointing out the hallowed site.   Of course
these were all chapels appertaining to Popish
times, and their numbers would seem to indicate,
that there has been formerly a far greater population than at present.   A similar inference may be
drawn, from the fact, that at no very distant date
whale's and seal's flesh formed a considerable part
of the people's food, as at the present day in
Faroë.

Only two ancient buildings, of any extent, are
to be found in Shetland, and both have been partially inhabited within the memory of the present
generation, but they are now roofless and rapidly
decaying.   One of these is the Castle of Scalloway,
an imposing, but not very extensive structure,

---

* " Viking," pronounced Vee-king.   Sea King as " *Vi-Sker-
ries*" means " *Sea-Skerries*."

built by a tyrannous governor, whose memory is justly execrated throughout the country, and who finally paid the penalty of his life for mal-administration. The other old castle is in Unst; but while the former is only a memento of oppression and chicanery,—of the latter, the following interesting legend is related on the spot:—

Muness is the south-east point of Unst; the land is verdant, and not very elevated. A little to the north is a very small and beautiful geo, so completely hidden and protected by the shores of the island, as to be almost undiscernible from the sea, and perfectly sheltered from the rudest blasts.

On a lovely mid-summer's night, towards the close of the sixteenth century, a small schooner-rigged vessel made her way to this retired haven. She was evidently armed, and was full of men, who by the help of two boats towed their ship into the geo, where she lay snugly anchored, and almost hidden.

The simple inhabitants of this part of Unst were greatly alarmed. They were totally unaccustomed to the visits of any sort of vessel, as the neighbouring coast is open, and exposed to heavy seas, when the wind is south or east. As for the geo, it had heretofore been considered inaccessible except to fishing-boats.

The men who landed at Muness from the strange schooner conducted themselves with a bold and fearless assurance, not at all in harmony with the ways of Shetlanders, yet they were by no means rude or mischievous. They paid handsomely for what they required from the inhabitants; but as they had no merchandise, or commodities to exchange, which might evidence their being traders or smugglers, the alternative was, they were—*Pirates ;* and each night the terrified natives retired to rest expecting they might all be plundered and massacred ere morning.

What then was their gratified surprise, when a few days after the vessel's arrival, some females and children were landed, and strolled for a while on the pebbly beach and smooth greensward slope of the Ness.

Two Muness girls who were looking after their cows, became unexpectedly confronted with this group of strangers, who essayed to hold with them a short converse; but as any dialect, except *Norse*, was most imperfectly known in this district, the intended intercourse was confined to a few sentences, in which Nature's universal language, expressed by tone and gesture, was alone intelligible. The girls reported to their friends, that they had distinguished two ladies, an elderly female attendant, and several fine boys and girls. One of the ladies was young, very beautiful, and still more,—" winsome." Supporting an elder lady on his arm, was a very tall and noble looking man, who though courteous enough, maintained a somewhat fierce and haughty air, to which the pistols and short sword he carried at his belt, perhaps in some degree contributed. A *pirate,* however, he could scarcely be, thus accompanied. The Shetlanders' terrors were at once ended, and the intention abandoned of giving public information against the strangers at the first opportunity.

The islands at this time were under great misrule; the people were *every where* and *every how* oppressed, and therefore had neither love for their governors, nor confidence in the laws. They were well enough satisfied, if tolerably secure from individual ill treatment; and perhaps, shrewdly considered, that one set of superiors was just as good as another, and might have even a better title to govern. Even if these strangers turned out to be foreign conquerors, the residents could hardly be worse off than they already were, as to the administration of law and equity. But they soon discovered that their free and easy friends belonged to Scotland, to whose government Shetland had become amenable, and so they doubted not it would turn out " all right in the end." Thus reasoned the Muness people, while their new acquaintances coolly began to erect a mansion on the slope of the shore, where it commanded a full view, not only of the geo where their schooner lay, and of the sea to a considerable distance, but of the Ness on one side, and the adjacent district of the island on the other.

There were plenty of rough stones on the beach hard by; many vigorous arms, and rude appliances were forthcoming to collect and build them up, and there was abundance of clay also at hand, so that in a very short time a strong and strange building was reared. The walls were many feet in thickness;

the lowest story, partly sunk, was vaulted over and
divided into a perfect labyrinth of dark recesses,
and narrow passages; one only tolerably sized
apartment was in the midst, where was a chimney
and fire-place large enough to roast an ox whole.
In this flat, and in the next above it, there were no
windows. A turret at each corner of the structure,
in the same style of solid masonry, contained stone
stairs leading to the second and third stories, in the
latter of which only was any provision for light
from without, though small round apertures either
for arms or observation pierced the massive walls
in many places. At the foot of the turret stairs,
were heavy oaken doors, thickly cramped with iron,
and kept closely secured with ponderous locks and
bars. One low door or postern, admitting to the
ground flat, was the only mode of ingress or egress
to this fortress mansion, which still displays in
wall and turret, stairs and vaults, all that has been
here described. Over the portal moreover, is to be
seen this inscription:—

> List ye to knaw this building quha began,
> Laurance the Bruce, he was that worthie man,
> Quha earnestlie his ayris, and affspring prayis.
> To help, and not to hurt, this wark alwayis.
> xv.xc.viii.

Laurence Bruce of Cultzmalindy, then, a Perth-
shire gentleman of property, was the leader of the
bold intruders at Muness,—the owner of the
schooner,—and father of the graceful and lovely
family.

In some clannish feud in his native country, he

had in single combat slain his opponent, and was compelled to fly, not from the strong arm of the law, but from the vengeance of the family of the man whose blood he had shed.

Bruce being well provided with money, obtained a vessel,—gathered a small band of sturdy retainers, and sailed for these remote islands, where having built and fortified a castle, which, as we have seen, he did after a fashion of his own, he concluded he should be safe from his enemies. Afterwards he obtained from the Udallers or ancient peasant proprietors of Unst, not only the ground on which he had raised his mansion, but several tracts of land besides, and then commenced a reign as landlord, judge, and farmer, sufficiently despotic, but by no means unjust. Occasionally he made voyages to Norway, where it was said he also purchased from the simple Udallers considerable landed property.

The Castle of Muness was always kept in a fortified condition, especially in its master's absence from the island. The females and children lived wholly in the upper flat, from which, however, to compensate for other evils, they enjoyed a beautiful view of the boundless, ever-changeful, but ever-cheerful sea,—sometimes in its glorious expanse of slumberous calm, but far oftener in its moods of fitful fury. The young people, who had never resided at any coast before, were delighted to watch the wild waves breaking in foam and thunder on the Ness, or whitening, as with a margin of snow, the several points of land within sight of their lattices. When Bruce was at home, his family were permitted to walk abroad, but only, as we saw at the first, accompanied by himself. In the evenings, he and his wife instructed their children in such branches of learning as were thought necessary at that day, especially music, in which they all excelled.

As soon as the castle had been made habitable, and furnished in such rude style as the circumstances admitted of, *The Dolphin*, Bruce's schooner, was sent to Scotland for some supplies,—an oversight we wonder to find him guilty of, since the opposite continent of Denmark or Holland would have furnished him with all he required.

The Shetlanders then lived almost entirely on animal food, such as fish, and the produce of their flocks and cattle, besides whales and seals' flesh. Circumscribed and scant were their arable land and crops, so that like all nations in an early stage of society, when regular commerce has not been established, they were at one time supplied with overflowing abundance, and quite as frequently subject to the horrors of famine.

Winter was approaching,—a season of scarcity was to be apprehended, and Laurence Bruce's family and dependents looked often and anxiously across the sea for the return of their vessel.

But there was one pair of beautiful eyes that gazed still more wistfully than those of all the rest. Marjory Bruce, the eldest of the family, had been early betrothed to a scion of the clan with whose chief her father had quarrelled and fought,—not indeed without provocation, for he had sought to do Bruce a wrong men rarely ever forgive.

As the heroine of our tale, Marjory, of course, ought to be described as lovely beyond compare. We have before noticed, that the Muness girls admired her greatly, so that one of them gladly became her attendant in the castle,—with permission, however, to sleep every night at her mother's. The truth of Marjory's grace and loveliness has been thus traditionally handed down to us, as something much more than common, indeed as quite worthy of a heroine. She was, moreover, ardent as she was amiable, and hopeful, even in her " castle prison, guarded by the sea," that her lover,—of whom she had been desired to think no more,— would discover her retreat, and effect some communication with her. Marvellous is the faith,— long-enduring, as unswerving,—which woman reposes in an absent lover! Pity it is ever misplaced! But so was not that of Marjory Bruce.

The Dolphin arrived at last deeply laden with rye and oatmeal, and also with many luxuries for the household. On the same evening, Hulda, the Shetland handmaid, delivered to her young mistress a missive from Scotland, which one of the men had confided to her. It proved to be neither letter nor flower, but a fragment of the hawk's plume from a Highland bonnet, and a small antique silver ring. On these tokens Marjory's heart reposed during the succeeding winter. Strange enough she never thought of questioning the bearer of her little packet, as she might have done,—one should say, *ought* to have done. But ere long she remarked, with uneasiness, which almost excluded other thoughts from her breast, that her father became more reserved towards her, apparently watching her narrowly; and when at length summer somewhat suddenly came, chasing away the gloom of a hard and stormy winter and spring, Bruce commanded that she should be confined wholly to one of the upper turret chambers!

In vain the lovely girl throwing herself at her stern father's feet, implored, at least to know her fault; he was not only imperious but implacable. We may as well, however, let the reader know, that the messenger of Malcolm M'Inroy, Marjory's betrothed, had, in a fit of intemperance, for which punishment was threatened, purchased his own immunity, by betraying to Bruce the fact, that M'Inroy had made a communication to his daughter, though he carefully concealed that *he* was the bearer of it.

Bruce,—or Cultzmalindy, as he was more generally called,—made but one short voyage to Bergen that season, and while absent, his castle was doubly garrisoned. Under all circumstances, indeed, the door was guarded night and day by a man fully armed, and other retainers, amounting to fifteen men at least, slept in the vaulted chambers below. There were also those whose employments and quarters were on board the Dolphin. The strong walls were proof against any appliances of war then known, and casements there were none, that might be reached. The captive in the

turret was visited once a-day by her father and
mother, and her attached handmaid, Hulda, who
then attended to all her comforts; and when the
father was away, as he entrusted the key of the
chamber to a fierce and surly fellow, Hulda sought
and obtained leave to share her dear young lady's
solitude for the time.

Marjory drooped, it may well be supposed, under
this treatment, for which she could but guess the
cause; yet so sweet and loving was her disposition,
she ever spoke contented-like, and even cheerily to
the other members of the family, when they were
able to converse a few minutes with her now and
then from the dark landing-place of the stairs,
above which her prison was situated. Her mother,
in whom the dutiful child might have expected a
powerful advocate, seems to have been entirely
submissive to the harsh sway of her lord, and made
no attempts in Marjory's behalf, farther than the
most tender and soothing caresses, and sedulous
care that her daughter should be supplied with
every indulgence likely to mitigate the hardships
of her penance.

Drearily passed a summer unusually bright and
propitious for this latitude, and autumn had again
arrived. The Dolphin was sent this time over to
Holland for the ordinary supplies, and Marjory
was given to understand, that she should be restored to at least partial freedom, as soon as the
vessel returned, and was laid up for the winter.
On this the gentle sorrowing maiden's spirits revived, and from the lofty and lonely lattice of her

tower, the Muness fishermen,—as they passed and
repassed on their way to their landing-place in the
geo,—could hear the strains of the lute or guitar,
accompanied by the performer's voice,—"just,"
said they, "like the prisoned bird that makes
sweet melody even in its cage."

About this time two men one day presented
themselves at the castle. They stated that they
were Dutch fishers from the Island of Yell, who
were about to return to their own country for
the winter, but having a few kegs of "strong
waters," and other commodities to dispose of,
wished to know if they might be admitted to bar-
gain for their goods. Bruce himself having spoken
outside to one of the men, and ascertained that he
was what he represented himself to be, gave the
required leave for their admission, the rather, that
he always encouraged this sort of traffic, almost
indeed the only commerce, carried on at the time
in Unst.

The strangers disposed profitably of their burdens,
and were then hospitably entertained. They in-
timated that their boat lay in the geo, close beneath
the castle, and as there would be tolerable moon-
light in the evening, they were in no great haste
to be gone. About the deepening twilight, two
more of their comrades arrived to enquire why they
were detained, and these new comers, the porter on
duty admitted,—it seems inadvertently,—without
question or orders. The visitors were carousing
with Bruce's men in the apartment over the kitchen,
with which it communicated by a trap stair, but

with no other part of the house; and the rites of hospitality were so much respected, that the master of the mansion withdrew to the upper chambers, to leave the visitors at the more perfect freedom. By the time the supper hour of the family had arrived, however, the guests had contrived to render the men of the castle thoroughly intoxicated, by drugging the " strong waters" they had brought with them, and on pretence of tasting, had induced the others to drink pretty freely.

It was about this hour that Hulda was accustomed to retire to the neighbouring cottage of her mother for the night. The same man who had previously employed her to carry his message to her mistress, and who had cherished and professed an ardent attachment to herself, she found was now watching for her, as if he hoped to be allowed as he sometimes was, to see her home; but on this occasion, as he was in fact the guard on duty, he only whispered eagerly, "Hulda darling, get this note to Miss Bruce somehow."

"Alas, how can I!" replied the girl, "no possible excuse I could invent would make the master let me to her now!"

"Ah, but Hulda my precious, you must; shove it under her door,—in by the key-hole,—any how."

"Andrew, thou know'st," rejoined Hulda, " I would serve my dear young lady with my heart,— my life.—I have ever told thee all she suffers,— God help me, if the master only knew! Is this for *her* good, Andrew?"

"Yes, yes, Hulda, for mercy's sake be quick! or evil will come of it,—bitter evil, my jewel!"

Hulda astonished at his agitation, and alarmed for her beloved mistress, parleyed no longer, but groped her way back to the single stair-case door that had been left open for her exit, and was not yet closed. A long circuit she had to make above, through galleries and chambers, ere she reached the steps that led still higher to the prison door of Marjory Bruce. In darkness and haste sped Hulda, but she was not afraid of her sounding footfall being heard, for Bruce and his family, as was their custom, were chanting in no contemptible strains, their evening hymns.

Marjory, just about to retire to her lonely couch, heard with surprise, that Hulda was at her door, and with some difficulty, comprehended that her faithful attendant had a message of importance for her. At once, then, imagining the Dolphin had arrived, the captive with great trepidation, and after several ineffectual efforts, received through the hey-hole of the thick door, the important billet, and Hulda hurried away in terror, fearing that the means of egress, might be in the interval barred against her. When she had rejoined her lover, he proposed even to abandon his post, that he might accompany her safely home.

"What will become of us if thou art missed Andrew?" remonstrated Hulda; but he only hurried her precipitately out, and then instead of going towards her home, he half persuaded,—half compelled her to accompany him to the beach, when

he explained to the bewildered affectionate girl the
intended proceedings of the night, and besought
her to fly with him and her young lady, and ulti-
mately to become his wife.

Meanwhile Marjory read her billet. It said, that
he whom she loved and trusted was without the
castle walls, and had heaped high beneath her window, straw and heather, on which she was implored to jump, and escape to liberty and love.

Had Marjory been acquainted with the extent
of that night's designs, (of which her deliverance
was but a part,) no power,—even that of early
and strong attachment,—could have induced her
to leave her father's roof; for the men then within
the walls, were emissaries of his mortal foe, resolved to destroy by treachery, both him and his
followers, since open force seemed likely to be
unavailing.

But Marjory suspecting nothing of all this, hesitated only till she should wrap herself in an ample
plaid, when she crept into the deep embrasure of
the latticed casement. Here, when she looked
down, the distance seemed so great, she faltered
and drew back, though the clearly rising crescent
moon, served to show her proposed deliverer, wildly
stretching his arms as if to receive her.

Marjory however felt that her safety demanded
farther means of assistance for her descent from a
height so considerable. She therefore tore her long
plaid in four strips, which she knotted together,
and then fastening one end round her waist, and
the other to the heavy oak post of her bed-place,

she slid herself over the window sill. It still required, that a knife fastened to a long rod, should be handed to her, wherewith to cut herself down, when she dropped in safety on the soft pile that had been placed to receive her. An eager thrilling greeting ensued between the young lovers, when they hasted to the boat, and found Andrew and Hulda, with a cousin of Malcolm's, and their men. Instantly they set sail with a light and favouring breeze, and having rounded the Ness, they stopped, as agreed on, to take in their four companions from the castle. Not finding them awaiting as they expected, and fearing for themselves the consequences of any delay, they thought it best to make for their sloop at once, supposing their followers would find no difficulty in afterwards rejoining them,—which, however, they never did!

To explain the proceedings of young M'Inroy, it is necessary to ask the reader to look back to the autumn of the preceding year, when Bruce's schooner had visited Scotland as previously mentioned.

It happened that Malcolm and one of his cousins, had business in a small town near the Firth of Forth. The latter in fact was expecting the arrival of a vessel from Denmark, wherein one of his uncles was returning from a diplomatic mission to that kingdom. Malcolm accompanied his cousin and chief, partly from the restless desire of change that often besets a baffled unhappy lover, and partly in the faint hope that he might find, in the course of his travel, some clue to the retreat of his beloved Marjory.

The gentlemen with their attendants, reached in the evening the chief *hostel* of the town alluded to, and according to the custom of the times, were accommodated, with guests of every degree, in the spacious kitchen. On one side of the ample fireplace, were already seated some sailor-like persons, one of whom Malcolm instantly thought he had seen before, and indeed soon persuaded himself that he was one of Cultzmalindy's followers, and a trusted one. With secret satisfaction young M'Inroy managed to draw this man's companions into conversation, when one of them inadvertently divulged, that they had lately come from the *Ultima Thulé* of Shetland. The speaker was checked by a signal from him whom Malcolm had recognised, and the latter now certain he was right, resolved at all hazards to make this man his own.

We need not stop to detail by what cajolery and bribes, plentifully mixed too with intimidation, Malcolm M'Inroy induced Andrew Bruce to tell of his master's having indeed sheltered in the wild isles of Shetland, of the strong-hold he had built, and the guarded watch he kept against force or surprisal.

Malcolm then explained to Andrew his passionate and faithful love for Marjory, and his resolution to attempt to see her. Plucking the feather from his bonnet, and a ring from a silver chain suspended round his neck,—the ring well known to his beloved, as a precious gift from his deceased mother,—he charged Andrew to convey them to Miss Bruce, engaging him by an ample donative, to assist the lover, should he find means of landing in Unst.

Andrew Bruce is represented as a brave and extremely handsome highlander, yet lacking in a highlander's proudest and holiest kept virtue,—fidelity to his chief. But, in extenuation, it may be explained, that he had been deeply irritated on more than one occasion by his master's overbearing temper and manners, in cases where he had reason to expect peculiar clemency and indulgence.

Next day after the interview with Andrew, Malcolm related to his cousin,—brother and successor to the chieftain unfortunately slain by Laurence Bruce,—the information he had received, who thereupon resolved to prosecute the vengeance, which, according to the creed of those days, justice demanded for a brother's blood. The kinsmen consulted deeply, the elder taking of the other the most solemn oath, that on condition of providing for Marjory's safety and union with her lover, Malcolm should not divulge to any one the plot to be developed, or interfere with its arrangements in any particular.

To the *latter* part of this agreement Malcolm M'Inroy most willingly acceded, for he felt he dared not be accessory to any harm towards the father of her he loved so fondly. To the probable result of the *former* clause of the compact, he was reconciled, by an irrepressible desire by any means to see his Marjory again, and the anxiety he had suffered on her account, since their sudden and unlooked for separation. He was, then, to have neither " art nor part" in his kinsman's scheme, indeed it was but partially explained to him, but he was to

accompany the expedition,—he might hope to meet
Marjory,—he might yet obtain her for his bride.
This was all he thought of, or cared for. Early
attached to the lovely playmate of his childhood,
the sudden feud of their respective relations, ought
to have, could have, no power to loosen her claim
on his affections and devotedness, and even his fiery
and vindictive cousin Adam, displayed but faint
and sneering opposition to these natural sentiments of a generous breast.

But ships, and men, and means were not at
everybody's command, at the era of which we are
writing. That winter passed without any opportunity presenting itself to the cousins M'Inroy, of
fulfilling their designs. Summer with its long
bright days, and clear brief nights, was not the time
to venture on an enterprise of revenge, and probably lawless violence; so it came to pass that the
year had revolved, ere the adventurers found themselves in a small sloop, coasting along Scotland.
Having crossed the Pentland Firth, in whose vexed
tide they had a narrow escape, they touched at
Orkney as a stage in their voyage, and then stretched
boldly across the North Sea, and passing near to
Fair Isle, came in sight of Shetland on its west
side. They had brought with them meal and other
merchandise, acceptable to the Shetlanders, by dis-
posing of which, as they proceeded, they expected
to cloak their real errand, and prevent all suspicion
or enquiry; and as a farther means to this end,
they dispensed as yet with the assistance of native
pilots. Thus they passed the noble bay of St

Magnus, and turned into Yell Sound, where they finally resolved to leave their sloop, and proceed in a boat to Unst.   They considered themselves fortunate in being here able to hire a Shetland fishing boat, and to obtain as guide the Dutch fisherman,—one of those who were accustomed to spend the summer in these islands in prosecution of their calling.   At length the two M'Inroy's with their pilot, and ten of their own men, on the evening referred to, reached the romantic geo below Muness Castle.   Their farther proceedings we have seen.

Marjory Bruce had hardly escaped from her lofty prison-chamber, when the castle within was filled with smoke and flames.

The treacherous guests had set fire in several places to the wainscoating and furniture of the apartment they had been admitted to ; but in attempting to retreat, the porter having, as we have shown, abandoned his place, they missed the dark door-way, and found themselves in the confused recesses of the ground-floor.   Here they wandered hopeless of escape, till the smoke became thick and suffocating.   We regret to add, the fatal catastrophe ;—the four men were smothered in the dark vaulted dungeons !

When Laurence Bruce and his family discovered the danger that threatened them, from the dense volumes of smoke ascending from the burning wood of his castle, the first thoughts of the mother and her children, were for the captive girl in the turret.   Thither accordingly they all rushed, and the rather, that it was still higher than the rest of

the building. Of course they instantly perceived
Marjory's escape, and the means by which it
had been effected. It looked like a providential
leading for themselves; and Bruce, with stern
and laudable composure, put forth all his gigantic
strength, until he had lowered from above, his
wife and children, in the identical way his eldest
daughter had descended. When they were all
in safety, at his command they proceeded for
shelter to the nearest cottage, and then he returned to seek his men, whom he found helplessly
intoxicated in the blazing room. With almost
superhuman exertions, he dragged some and assisted others, to one of the turret stairs, where
they were comparatively safe; and then finding
himself nearly exhausted, he escaped as his family
had done before.

From the description we gave of the construction
of the castle, it will be easy to comprehend, that from
the scantiness of wood-work, as well as its freshness,
the flames did not make great progress; indeed
they soon stayed of their own accord, without in-
juring either roof or stairs. The damage was soon
afterwards repaired, and Laurence Bruce and his
family inhabited it for many years in freedom and
security, as he was never again molested in any
way.

It was only about three years after these events,
that Hulda, a youthful and sorrowing widow, returned to Muness, for which in her exile she had
sorely pined. She was the bearer of dutiful letters and costly presents, from Marjory and her

husband, to the circle at the castle. Bruce had relented, and the offending, but now completely happy pair were pardoned. Indeed the asperities of his nature seemed from that night to have been almost completely smoothed, so shocked had he been, when he discovered in the vaults of his dwelling, the sacrifice of human life he had indirectly been the means of causing.

The Unst people then began to learn and cultivate the use of the English language. Moreover, they lived peaceably and prosperously under Cultzmalindy's sway, and the name of Bruce, as a Christian one, for both men and women, is, to this day, most common in the island.

THE END.